Mahfuz, Najib, 1912-

The search

$20.00

	DATE DUE		
APR 21 2007			
JUN 11 2011			

© THE BAKER & TAYLOR CO.

THE
SEARCH

Naguib Mahfouz
THE
SEARCH

Translated by
Mohamed Islam
Edited by
Magdi Wahba

DOUBLEDAY
New York London Toronto Sydney Auckland

F

6-91 BT 2000

PUBLISHED BY DOUBLEDAY
a division of Bantam Doubleday Dell Publishing Group, Inc.
666 Fifth Avenue, New York, New York 10103

DOUBLEDAY and the portrayal of an anchor with a dolphin
are trademarks of Doubleday, a division of Bantam Doubleday
Dell Publishing Group, Inc.

*All of the characters in this book are fictitious,
and any resemblance to actual persons, living or dead,
is purely coincidental.*

The English translation of *The Search* was first published
by The American University in Cairo Press in 1987.
First published in Arabic as *al-Tariq* in 1964.
Protected under the Berne Convention.
The Doubleday edition is published by arrangement with
The American University in Cairo Press.

Library of Congress Cataloging-in-Publication Data
Maḥfūẓ, Najīb, 1911–
   [Ṭarīq, English]
   The search / Naguib Mahfouz; translated by Mohamed Islam;
   edited by Magdi Wahba. — 1st Doubleday ed.
        p.   cm.
   Translation of: al-Ṭarīq.
   Originally published: Cairo: American University Press, 1987.
   I. Wahba, Magdi. II. Title.
PJ7846.A46T313   1991   90-24347
892'.736—dc20   CIP
ISBN 0-385-26459-3
ISBN 0-385-26460-7 (pbk.)

THE
SEARCH

CHAPTER ONE

Tears filled his eyes. In spite of his control over his emotions and the repugnance he felt at weeping before these men, he was quite overcome. With moist eyes he looked at the corpse as it was removed from the coffin and carried to the open grave, the dead body seemingly weightless in its white shroud. Oh, how you've wasted away, Mother.

The scene faded and he could see only darkness, and the dust stung his nostrils, and the unpleasant stench of the men around him filled the air.

The wailing of the women, mingled with the sting of the dust, utterly disgusted him, and he moved forward, leaning over the open grave, but a hand pulled him back and a voice said, "Remember your God."

He was repulsed by the touch and cursed the man inwardly. That man's a pig like the rest of them. But then the awe of the moment roused him with a pang of remorse and he said, "A quarter of a century of love, tenderness, care, all gone, swallowed up by the earth as though it had never existed."

A wailing heralded the entrance of a group of blind men who surrounded the grave and sat cross-legged. He felt eyes gazing intently upon him and others stealing an occasional glance. He knew what these looks meant and stretched his lean body in stubborn defiance. They must be wondering why he was so strange in his appearance and dress, as though he were not one of them. Why did his mother remove him from his environment, then abandon him?

They have not come here to pay their condolences, but rather to gloat over you.

The gravedigger and his assistant appeared from below and proceeded vigorously to fill the grave with loose earth. The blind men were chanting on cue from their leader.

She will be truly lonely. What do these pigs have to say? Reverence, covering their faces like a summer cloud. He became impatient, craving the solitude of his house so he could meditate on his situation. Embarrassing questions will be put to his mother in the darkness of the grave. None of these devils will be of any help to her then. "But your time will come!"

The sounds died down, indicating the end of the ceremony, and the gravedigger took a few steps toward him but was stopped by the man standing on his right. "Let me deal with this. I know these people." He felt revulsion again, but as he realized that it was all over, his sense of loneliness overcame all else. He cast one last look at the grave, feeling at peace with its orderly appearance. Through the bars of the window he could see the creepers growing on the wall of the tomb. His mother, God rest her soul, was fond of the good life, but now all she had left was the grave.

The people moved slowly to offer him their condolences. First the women, who despite their weeping and wailing and mourning dress could not hide the licentious look in their eyes; then the men, drug peddlers, ruffians, hustlers, pimps, all muttering incoherent words of condolence. He looked at them all coldly, knowing full well that the feeling was reciprocated.

On his way home a refreshing breeze fanned him, carrying with it the fragrance of spring. His house on Nabi Danial Street was the scene of a happy, comfortable period in his life. However, the only signs of comfort remaining were the large hall and an abandoned water pipe under his mother's empty bed.

He sat on the balcony overlooking the intersection of Nabi Danial and Saad Zaghlul streets, smoking a cigarette. His attention was drawn to a flat across the street; foreigners lived there, and preparations were being made for a party. He could see a man and a woman embracing, rather inappropriate for that early time of the day.

He decided that as of today he would know life as it really was. He was lonely, without friends, work, or family, and he was left with nothing but a dreamlike hope. He must as of this moment fend for himself; that was previously his mother's domain, and he had been free to enjoy life to the fullest. Only yesterday thoughts of death could not have been further from his mind. It was yesterday, too, at about the same time, that the carriage had arrived bringing his mother home. He led her into the house, the house she had prepared for her son. She was weak and haggard, looking thirty years older than her fifty-odd years. That's how he remembered Basima Omran, as she was when she came home the previous day after having spent five years in jail.

"Your mother is through, Saber."

Carrying her effortlessly in his arms, he said, "Nonsense, you are in the prime of your youth."

She lay down on the bed fully clothed, leaned over to look in the mirror, and repeated, "Your mother is through, Saber. Who would believe that this is Basima Omran's face?"

How true. A round, handsome face, and the pink coloring of a ripening apple. Her laughter that had reverberated through every drawing room in Alexandria now failed to cause the slightest ripple on her large, fat body.

"May God curse sickness and disease."

Wiping her face, despite the cool weather, she said, "It's not sickness, but jail. I fell ill in jail. Your mother wasn't made for

3

jails. They said it was my liver, my blood pressure, then my heart, curse them. Can I ever again be what I was?"

"And even better, with rest, and medicine."

"And money?"

He winced and said nothing.

"How much have you got left?"

"Very little."

"I was wise to register the house at Ras el-Tin in your name; otherwise they would have taken that, too."

"But I sold it when I ran out of money. I told you at the time."

She groaned and placed her hand on her forehead. "Oh, my head, I wish you hadn't sold the house. You had a lot of money; I wanted you to lead the good life, to live like the aristocracy. I wanted to leave you a fortune, but . . ."

"Everything was lost in one stroke."

"Yes, may God forgive them, a mean revenge from a mean man, a man who enjoyed my wealth, then dropped me for a worthless slut. Suddenly he remembered the call of duty, law, and honor and discarded me, the bastard. I spat on him in court."

She asked for a cigarette; he lit one for her, saying, "It's better that you don't smoke now. Did you smoke in there?"

"Cigarettes, hashish, opium, but I always worried about you." She drew on the cigarette breathlessly, wiped her damp face and neck, and said, "What about your future, my boy?"

"How should I know? There's nothing for me to do but become a ruffian, a hustler or a pimp."

"You?"

"I know, you taught me a better life, but I'm afraid that won't do me any good."

"You weren't made for that kind of life."

"What else can I do in this world?" Then with sudden rage he exclaimed, "How my enemies gloated when you were away."

"Saber. Avoid anger. It's anger that sent me to jail; it would have been easier to appease that scoundrel who betrayed me."

"Everywhere I find people I'd like to crush."

"Let them say what they want, but don't use your fists."

Clenching his hands, he growled, "If it weren't for these fists I'd have been humiliated everywhere I went; no one dared mention a word about you when you were in jail."

She blew out the smoke angrily and said, "Your mother is far more honorable than their mothers. I mean it. They don't know, but if it weren't for their mothers my business would have floundered!"

Saber smiled, in spite of the oppressive atmosphere. His mother continued: "They're very clever at fooling people with their appearance, cars, clothes, expensive cigarettes. Well-spoken, smelling good, but I know them as they really are, I know them in the bedroom, naked except for their defects. I have endless stories about them, those dirty, sly bastards. Before the trial, many of them contacted me and urged me with great persistence not to mention their names at the trial, and in return they promised me freedom. Such people have no right to speak ill of your mother, for she is far more honorable than their mothers, wives, and daughters. Believe me, if it weren't for them I would be out of business."

The smile returned to his lips.

"Where have those laughing, carefree days gone?" She sighed. "I loved you with all my heart; everything I had was at your disposal. I let you live here in this lovely house far from my world. If I ever wronged you it was unknowingly. Your looks and elegance are unequaled, but you must avoid losing your temper or worry about what's happened to me." Her sadness was contagious.

He said softly, "Everything will be just as it was."

"As it was . . . I'm finished. The Basima of days long ago will never return; my health would not permit it, and neither would the police."

He looked at the floor. "Very little of the price of the house is left."

"What is there to do? You must maintain the standard of living I have accustomed you to."

"I've never known you to lose hope before."

"Only this once."

"Then I must either work or kill."

She put out her cigarette and closed her eyes as if trying to concentrate on a single idea.

"There must be a way out," continued Saber.

"Yes, I've given the matter much thought in jail."

For the first time his confidence in his mother was shaken.

"Yes," she continued, "I've thought about it a lot, and I am now convinced that I have no right to keep you here, since it is no longer good for you."

He looked at her, a questioning glance in his dark eyes.

Then with a tone of defeat she whispered, "You don't understand. The government took you away from me at the same time that they confiscated my wealth. I don't have the right to own you either. I knew that the day they sentenced me." She was silent for a while, utter despair on her face. "Saber, this means that you must leave me," she said.

"Where to?" he asked resentfully.

"To your father," she replied in a barely audible voice.

He raised his eyebrows in bewilderment and cried, "My father . . ."

She nodded.

"But he's dead. You told me he died before I was born."

"I told you so. But it wasn't true."

"My father, alive . . . Incredible . . . My father . . . alive."

She looked at him with sudden disdain as he continued: "My father alive . . . Why did you hide this from me?"

"Yes, the hour of reckoning has come." She sighed.

"No, no. But I've got a right to know."

"What father could have done for you all that I've done, your happiness . . . ?"

"I don't deny this at all . . ."

"Then don't reproach me and start searching for him."

"Searching?"

"Yes. I'm talking about a man whom I married thirty years ago, and now I don't know anything about him."

In a calmer vein but still bewildered, he asked, "Mother, what does all this mean?"

"It means that I'm trying to show you the only way out of your dilemma."

"But he might be dead."

"Or alive."

"Must I waste my life, then, looking for someone I'm not even sure exists?"

"You'll never be sure unless you find out. Anyway, it's better than staying as you are with no work and no hope."

"It's a very strange and unenviable situation!"

"Your only alternative is to become a hustler, a crook, a pimp, or a murderer. So you must do what must be done."

"How can I find him?"

She sighed, and an even greater sadness fell upon her. "His name is on your birth certificate, Sayed Sayed el-Reheimy." Her eyes grew misty as she continued: "He fell in love with me thirty years ago. That was in Cairo."

"Cairo ... Then he's not even in Alexandria."

"I know that your real problem will be to find him."

"Why didn't he try to find me?"

"He doesn't know about you."

A look of resentment and indignation crept into his eyes. "Wait," she said, "don't look at me like that. Listen to the rest of it. He is a man of means in every sense of the word. At the time he was a student, but even then he had considerable means and prestige."

He looked at her with increasing interest but somewhat distantly.

"He loved me. I was a beautiful, lost girl. He kept me secretly, in a golden cage."

"He married you?"

"Yes. I still have the marriage certificate."

"He divorced you?"

She sighed, "I ran away."

"You ran away?"

"I ran away after some years. I was pregnant. I ran away with a man from the gutter."

"Unbelievable," he muttered, shaking his head.

"Now you are going to blame me for your problem."

"I'm not blaming you for anything. But didn't he look for you?"

"I don't know. I ran away to Alexandria and never heard any more about him. Many times I expected to see him in one of my establishments, but I never set eyes on him again."

He laughed coldly and said, "And thirty years later you send me to look for him."

"Despair drives us to do even stranger things. You'll have the marriage certificate to help you. Also the wedding photograph. You'll see the striking resemblance."

"Strange that you kept the certificate and photograph."

"I was thinking of the picture. I was a poor girl living with a hustler, and when I became successful my intentions of avenging you were realized."

"And yet you never got rid of the rest of your memories."

She wiped her face and neck impatiently and said, "I intended to many times but changed my mind, as though I had a premonition of what would happen."

He paced back and forth, then stopped in front of her bed. "What if after all my efforts he denies me?"

"Who can deny you after seeing the photograph?"

"Cairo is a big city, and I've never been there before."

"Who says he's in Cairo? He might be in Alexandria, Assiut, or Damanhour. I have no idea. Where is he today? What is he doing? Is he married or single? God only knows."

He waved his arm angrily. "And how am I supposed to find him?"

"I know it won't be easy. But it's also not impossible. You know some police officers and lawyers. No prominent personality is unknown in Cairo."

"I'm afraid that my money might run out before I find him."

"That is why you must start at once."

He thought for a moment, then asked, "Is he worth all that effort?"

"Without the least doubt. You will find the life you want with him. You won't suffer the indignities of work or be forced to lead a life of crime."

"And if I find him poor? Weren't you extremely rich?"

"I assure you that money is only one of his assets. It's true that I was rich, but I never provided you an honorable life, and all you did was go about using your fists to defend your mother's and your own honor."

I must be dreaming, he thought. "Do you really believe that I'll find him?"

"Something tells me that he is alive, and that if you don't despair, you'll find him."

He shook his head, torn between bewilderment and hopelessness. "Should I really start searching for him? If my enemies know of this, won't they treat me as an insane freak?"

"And what will they say if they find you pimping? You have no alternative but to look for him." She closed her eyes, muttering about how exhausted she was, so he begged her to sleep, saying that they would resume their talk tomorrow. He took off her shoes and covered her, but she tossed off the cover with a nervous gesture and fell into a deep sleep punctuated by light snoring.

He awoke at nine o'clock next morning after a restless, sleepless night. He went to her room to wake her, and found his mother dead. Had she passed away in her sleep, or did she cry out in the night? An unheeded cry. No matter. Here she was, dead, in the same clothes as those in which she had left prison the day before. He looked closely at the wedding photograph. The only evidence of the existence of a father thirty years ago. How true. He was the image of his father. A handsome, virile-looking man, his tarboosh slightly tilted to the right, enhancing an already impressive figure.

The guests had started to arrive at the neighbors', the sound of music blending with the chants of the Qur'an in the dead woman's bedroom.

Where is reality, and where is dream? Your mother, whose last words are still echoing in your ears, now lies dead. Your dead father is seeking resurrection. And you, penniless, persecuted, tarnished with crime and sin, looking for a miracle that will lead you to a life of honor, freedom, and peace of mind.

CHAPTER TWO

Better to let the matter remain secret for the moment. Should he despair of the search, he could seek aid from his acquaintances. He'd start with Alexandria, although it was unlikely that someone like his father would be in Alexandria without his mother's knowing about it.

The telephone directory for a start. The letter S, Sayed el-Reheimy. Aha ... if only luck were on his side. Sayed Sayed el-Reheimy, owner of el-Manshiya bookshop. Very unlikely for a person of his father's social condition. In any case, el-Manshiya was an area worked by his mother for more than a quarter of a century. Still, this might be a useful clue.

The bookshop owner was a man over fifty, bearing no resemblance to the photograph. Covering his mother's face, he showed him the picture.

"No, I don't know this man," said the bookshop owner.

Saber explained that the photograph was taken thirty years before.

"I don't remember seeing him."

"Is he perhaps a relative?"

"We are Alexandrians, and all my relatives live here. Some of my relatives on my mother's side live in the countryside. Why are you looking for this man?"

He hesitated a moment, then said quickly, "He's an old friend of my deceased father. Do any of the Reheimys live elsewhere?"

The man looked at him suspiciously and said, "El-Reheimy is my grandfather, and there are only my sister and me."

There was no other course but to be patient. He had only two hundred pounds, and these were dwindling away with every passing hour. When they were gone, so went the hope of an honorable life. His eyes ached from scrutinizing every passerby. He consulted a lawyer of his acquaintance, who suggested that his father might have an unlisted number. "Ask the local Sheikh el-Hara,"* he suggested.

"My father is an important man," retorted Saber indignantly.

"Strange things can happen in thirty years. I was going to suggest that you ask about him in the various jails."

"Jails!"

"Why not? A jail is like a mosque, open to all. Sometimes people go to jail for noble reasons." With a short laugh, the lawyer continued: "Let's start with the registry offices, then the jails and the property registrars. If there is no trace there, we have no alternative but to ask the local sheikhs."

Saber rejected the idea of an advertisement in the paper. This would give his enemies an opportunity to make fun of him. The advertisement would have to wait until he left the city. He made the rounds of the local sheikhs, from one end of Alexandria to the other.

"What does he do?"

"I don't know anything about him except that he is a well-known personality and of ample means. This is a photograph of him taken thirty years ago."

"Why are you looking for him?"

"He's an old friend of my father's and I've been asked to look for him."

"Are you sure he's still alive?"

*Literally "The Elder of the Alley." He is a person who has lived for a long time in a particular quarter of the city and who is relied upon by the authorities to assist in maintaining a register of births, deaths, and addresses in the quarter.

"I'm not sure of anything."

"How did you know he's in Alexandria?"

"Only a hunch, nothing more."

Then the final answer would resound like the clanging of a cell door, "Sorry, we don't know him." He did not cease his scrutiny of every passerby, in a continuous whirlpool of searching, without success. The raindrops forced him to retreat from the seashore and move on to Miramar. He looked up to the late afternoon sky with the first shades of darkness gently edging away the remaining daylight. A voice cried out in welcome, "Come."

He shook hands and sat down.

"I wasn't able to pay you my condolences, but I waited until you came to Le Canard. Everyone is asking about you." The rain had stopped. He stood up, making some excuse about an appointment. She got up and said softly, "Are you in financial straits?"

So they've begun talking!

Temptingly she continued: "Someone like you should never be in want of money."

He shook hands coldly and left. Someone like you should never be in want of money. The call of the madam. That's just what your enemies want. I'd rather be dead. What's left in Alexandria?

The palm reader; but nothing new.

The sheikh, all-knowing perhaps. He visited him in his ground-floor room, shuttered and musty. The sheikh, sitting cross-legged on the floor lost in thought, said, "Seek and ye shall find." The sound of waves seemed to augur a promising start. "A search as tedious as the winter nights," the sheikh added. Every day is like a year, and at what expense! "You shall obtain what you seek."

With a startled voice: "What is it that I'm seeking?"

"He is waiting for you impatiently."

"Does he know about me?"

"He's waiting for you"

Maybe his mother didn't tell him everything.

"Then, he is alive!"

"Thanks be to God."

"Where do I find him? That's what I really want to know."

"Patience."

"I can't be patient indefinitely."

"You've just begun."

"In Alexandria?"

The sheikh closed his eyes. "Patience, patience," he murmured.

"You've told me nothing," retorted Saber angrily.

"I've told you everything," replied the sheikh.

He walked out cursing and was greeted by the introductory rumbles of a thunderstorm. He decided to sell his furniture and leave for Cairo. He had already sold the costly objects in order to maintain his expensive tastes and extravagant living. He hated having the secondhand dealers and buyers come to his flat, so he paid a visit to "Madam" Nabawiya, a close friend of his mother's, and the only one in that circle he did not dislike.

"I'll be glad to buy your furniture, but why are you leaving?" she asked, offering him a puff from her narghileh.

"I'll make a new life for myself in Cairo, away from all this."

"May God have mercy on her soul. She loved you and ruined you for any other kind of life."

He understood what she meant and said, "I'm no longer fit for this kind of life."

"What will you do in Cairo?"

"I have a friend who promised he'd help me."

"Believe me, our work is suited only to the proud."

He spat in a large incense bowl. That was his response.

Alexandria faded in the distance as the train sped south toward Cairo. A quarter of a century of memories faded away in the autumn twilight, enveloped in dark clouds heralding November with its cold winds blowing through half-deserted streets. He bade a silent farewell to the city, wondering what the future held in store for him. His sole companions for the journey were his thoughts, thoughts about his father. The questions he had asked, the evasive answer from his mother. He had always assumed that he was the product of a moment of pleasure in any one of the numerous brothels. A bastard.

The sudden din of the Cairo station cut through his thoughts. His immediate impulse was to board the next train for Alexandria. But he thought better of it, left his luggage at the station, and walked out into the late afternoon sun. He was struck by all the appurtenances of a big city, the cars, buses, pedestrians, street vendors, noise, wide streets, noise, narrow streets, noise. Contradiction and contrasts everywhere. Even the weather, the hot rays of a sun struggling to the last before setting, and a pleasant cool breeze waiting to take over after the struggle was inevitably finished.

He eventually found himself in an arcaded street across from the Cairo Hotel, an establishment that looked like it was within his means. And as though to emphasize this fact, a beggar was sitting cross-legged near the doorway chanting a religious song. The street was crowded with shops on both sides, and piles of merchandise were strewn all over the sidewalks.

The hotel was an old building with sand-colored walls rising four floors above him. An arched doorway led into a long corridor with a stairway at the end. In the middle of the corridor stood the reception desk presided over by a seated old man, and beside him stood a woman. What a woman! He felt an immediate awakening of long-dormant desires and memories lost in the fog of time. The sound and smell of the sea and moments of insane passion, inflamed by the darkness of night. An intimate relationship sprang up between him and the hotel; it was as though they were destined to meet.

He crossed the street and entered with a burning curiosity. The beautiful dark girl, her almond eyes flashing with temptation and seduction. A clinging, pale-colored dress, long fingernails suggesting an exciting animal desire.

She reminded him of her. Ten, maybe more years ago, the name long forgotten but the moment recaptured in its entirety. The girl of long past was of no consequence, but here she was now, bringing back the past, calling out, just as his father was doing. A call from the dead that brought him from the sea to this exciting, teeming city. She gave him a fleeting glance full of meaning, then quickly turned her face toward the hotel lounge on her right. Saber walked up to the desk, where the old man was bent over a large register, a magnifying glass in his trembling hand. The old man did not notice him, so he stole a glance at the woman and assured himself of the promise he had first detected. She glanced back at him with a touch of scorn and nudged the old man, upon which Saber immediately greeted him. "Good evening, sir."

The old man raised his head to display a deeply lined face with a prominent hooked nose. The look in his pale eyes indicated a total lack of interest in the whys and wherefores of this world.

"I'm looking for a room," Saber said.

"Twenty piasters a night."

"And if I stay for two weeks?"

"Twenty piasters is worth nothing nowadays."

"I might stay for a month or more."

The old man gave up the bargaining and murmured, "As you wish."

Saber gave his name and place of origin, and when asked about his occupation simply said, "I have private means." He gave the old man his identity card, stealing glances at the woman while the man was busy writing down the details. Their eyes met, but he failed to read the meanings he had first seen. Nevertheless, he convinced himself that she was that girl of his past. Once more the smell of the sea stung his nostrils as well as the scent of the carnations that had adorned her hair. All of a sudden he was optimistic about the success of his mission and did not doubt for a moment that this woman was ready and willing. She appeared to be disinterested, but an enchantress lay beneath that cool façade.

The old man returned the identity card, saying, "You are from Alexandria?"

He nodded and smiled, and said slyly, looking to the girl, "I bet you like Alexandria?"

The old man smiled, but the girl, contrary to his expectations, did not appear even to have heard, so he quickly asked, "Did you ever know Sayed Sayed el-Reheimy?"

"It's not improbable that I did."

Saber became keenly interested, forgetting the girl. "Where and when?"

"I can't remember; I'm not sure."

"But he is an important man."

"I've known many, but now I don't remember one."

His optimism increased. He glanced at the girl and saw a look of doubt and mockery in her eyes, as though she were asking why a man of private means should stay in this hotel. It didn't bother him. The truth would appear when she discovered the reason for his being there. And she would find out sooner or later.

Did she remember him? He felt the long fingernails dig into his flesh after the long chase along the Corniche in Alexandria. The chase that ended in the dark with the sea breeze blowing over their naked bodies. But where was her father then? And when did he move to Cairo to run this hotel?

The woman called out, "Mohamed el-Sawi."

An old man stood up from his seat near the door and answered her call. He was very dark, short, and lightly built. He wore a gray-striped galabiya and a white skullcap.

She pointed to Saber and said, "Room thirteen."

Saber smiled at the number. He excused himself and went back to the station to get his luggage. When he returned, he followed Mohamed el-Sawi to his room on the third floor. A middle-aged porter, moving far too quickly for his profession, carried his bags. The porter had small, closely set eyes and a very small head that gave him an air of naïveté.

"What's your name?" asked Saber.

"Aly Seriakous."

The way he said it told Saber that he was a man who could be bought.

"Is the old man at the desk the owner of the hotel?"

"Yes, Mr. Khalil Abul Naga."

He was about to ask about the woman when he warned himself that naïveté can be a two-edged sword.

When he was alone he looked over his surroundings. The immediate impression was that of age. High ceiling and a four-poster bed. His father must have enjoyed such surroundings when he made love to his mother. He looked out the window onto a square at the northern end of the street. Children were splashing about in the fountain in the center of the square. He switched on the light and sat on the old divan, closing his eyes. Sexual fantasies, intermingled with dreams of finding his father, swept over him.

He could hear the call of those almond eyes. She might now be thinking of him and asking herself about the reason for his presence. There was no doubt that she was the girl. He could hear her voice above the din of the festival, telling him sharply not to come near her in this manner.

You had replied haughtily that no girl had ever spoken to you like that before. She retorted that she did and would repeat it. She left with a vulgar-looking woman, the breeze caressing her hair. Where was Mr. Khalil then? Your eyes met today more than once, and the looks were full of meaning. But no hint of memories past. No hint of long talks by the sea near the overturned fishing boats, conversations that disguised passion and powerful desires. A stolen kiss followed by a friendly tussle. Then you cried out, "One day I'll pull out those long fingernails!"

As to the long chase which ended in the dark, that was a total victory, a victory that was followed by disappearance and a long silence. Then sorrow that lasted for a long time until your mother moved from one quarter to the other, and ended in the elegant flat in the Nabi Danial district. Who knows? This hotel might have some connection with that dark night and the girl with carnations in her hair. This woman arouses a tempest of passion in your veins. And you need moments of warmth and passion to ease your search and alleviate the pangs of loneliness. And then, when the miracle occurs, you will cry out, "I'm Saber, Saber Sayed Sayed el-Reheimy! Here is my birth certificate and here is the marriage certificate, and look carefully at this photograph."

Then you will open your arms and all evil thoughts and doubts will vanish forever.

You have become a lady in every sense of the word. Where is that girl covered with salty spray? Where is that pure virgin smell?

CHAPTER THREE

He rose early, after only three hours' sleep, feeling surprisingly refreshed.

Opening the window, he saw a world he had never seen before. The familiar Alexandria scene, the buildings and usual morning sights were replaced by those of an alien world. Even the air he breathed was different. The strange surroundings conjured up an image of his father, the object of his search. Aly Seriakous brought in his breakfast, which he wolfed down hungrily. When the servant returned to take the tray Saber asked him, "Who was the girl sitting next to Mr. Khalil yesterday?"

"His wife."

This was unexpected. With what sounded like shocked indignation he asked, "From Alexandria?"

"I have no idea"

"When did Mr. Khalil buy the hotel?"

"I don't know. I've only been working here for five years."

"Was he married then?"

"Yes."

There was no doubt about it. She was the girl from his past. The old man bought her from that vulgar woman and made her a lady. But he must concentrate on his search, before the money runs out. He left his room and went downstairs, and found Mr. Khalil talking to Mohamed el-Sawi, the doorman. Some of the hotel residents were in the lounge, reading newspapers or drinking coffee, and some were just chatting together. He walked up to Mr. Khalil, greeted him, and asked for the telephone directory.

Sayed . . . Sayed . . . Sayed . . . Sayed . . . Aha. Sayed Sayed el-Reheimy. There it is . . . His heart beat faster. A doctor and professor at the Faculty of Medicine. Now that's something! He could not contain his joy, and cried out, "It seems that the Almighty is on my side."

The old man looked up with his weak, distant look. "It looks as though I shall succeed in what I came for," Saber continued.

"Success is a wonderful thing," murmured the old man.

Just as you succeeded in possessing that beautiful girl!

The old man was still looking at him, with mounting curiosity. "I'm looking for a man. Someone who means the world to me," Saber explained.

"No one comes to this hotel to stay. They always have some specific mission or particular purpose that takes them a day, a week, or a month to fulfill, then they leave," said the old man.

"That's normal," replied Saber.

"That's why even though they share the same roof and have their meals together, they never get to know each other."

"I imagine that your work must be interesting," said Saber, trying to maintain the conversation.

"Absolutely not!"

What about the vicissitudes of fate! The girl, for example! He heard footsteps behind him, and she appeared wearing a black skirt and red blouse and, around her head, a white polka-dotted scarf. His heart almost stopped beating. The look in her eyes showed the promise of virgin land! The smell of sea breeze hit his nostrils once more. The doorman stood and picked up a battered gray suitcase. The old man raised his head from the hotel register.

"Are you leaving now?"

"Yes, I'll see you later. Goodbye." She left the hotel followed by Mohamed el-Sawi. You are truly a mystery, Khalil! That face of yours, expressionless like a death mask. Saber got up with apparent calmness, excused himself, and walked out of the hotel. His eyes scanned the street. There they are! Walking toward the square. He hurried after them, quickly catching up. The doorman turned around, questioningly. With an apologetic smile Saber asked, "Excuse me, Mr. Mohamed. Can you tell me the way to Azhar Square?"

The woman looked at him in surprise. The doorman started to point out the directions. He pretended to listen, frequently stealing glances. The promising, provocative look was in her eyes. He was about to ask her about the carnations in her hair, the salty sea breeze, and the naked darkness. The doorman had stopped talking. He thanked him and left them. Where was she going with her watchdog? Was he perhaps overly presumptuous? He had always been forward. But perhaps this time it might ruin everything.

Arriving at the address, he found the doctor's assistant, who told him that the doctor usually came around noontime. He sat down and waited. Was this the place where his father worked? Fear, despair, hope, anxiety all came crowding in. What would he do if his father denied him? He would fight for his rights to the bitter end! In his excitement he suddenly realized that he didn't know what the doctor specialized in. He walked out of the waiting room and approached the assistant.

"Please, what branch of medicine does the doctor specialize in?"

"He is a cardiologist."

"I just wanted to make sure. You see, I'm from Alexandria."

He realized how foolish he must have sounded, but he didn't care. "Do you have any idea as to the doctor's age?" he asked.

"I have no idea," replied the assistant with surprise.

"But you can guess, roughly?"

"He is a professor at the Faculty of Medicine."

"Is he married?"

"Yes, and he has a son, who is a medical student."

Now, that is an obstacle! The family will certainly have something to say about the new member coming from the brothels. Nevertheless, he was determined.

The patients started arriving and the waiting room filled up. His turn came. Anxious and full of doubt, he walked into the consulting room. The face bore no resemblance to the photograph. He sat opposite the doctor and started answering his questions.

"My name is Saber Sayed Sayed el-Reheimy."

"Then you must be my son," said the doctor with a loud laugh.

"Actually, I'm not here for your professional advice."

The doctor looked at him questioningly.

"I am looking for Sayed Sayed el-Reheimy."

"You are looking for me?"

"I don't know. But please take a look at this photograph."

The doctor looked at it carefully and shook his head.

"This is not your photograph?"

"Definitely not," he answered with a laugh. "Who is that beautiful woman?"

"Perhaps one of your relatives? It was taken thirty years ago."

"No, no."

"You are from the Reheimy family?"

"My father is Sayed el-Reheimy. He worked at the post office."

"Are there any other branches of your family?"

"No. My family is a very small one."

He stood up, despair lining his face. "I am sorry to have troubled you. But maybe you've heard of someone with that name?"

"I don't know anyone of that name. What exactly are you looking for?"

"I'm looking for Sayed Sayed el-Reheimy, the man in this photograph, taken thirty years ago."

"He might be anywhere. In any case, I'm not an authority on missing persons," said the doctor in a tone that indicated the end of the interview.

He walked into the first bar he found and ordered a brandy. He had to start all over again. The telephone directory was nothing more than a cruel mockery. The optimism that had swept over him when he saw Khalil's wife was now fading fast. He remembered his fruitless search in Alexandria, the registry offices, the local sheikhs. But here in Cairo he knew no one. Perhaps it was best to place an advertisement in the paper. He looked at the old barman and asked, "Do you know a Sayed Sayed el-Reheimy?"

"Yes, he is a doctor in a building not far from here."

"No. Not that one. He is an important person. A man of considerable means."

The barman, a foreigner, repeated the name a couple of times, and then said, "I don't recall any of my customers with such a name."

"Have you ever tried looking for someone without knowing where to start?"

"A lost son since the war?"

Saber shook his head.

"But the war is long over. And everyone's fate is now known."

"Rather lost, than dead." Saber asked the barman about the *Sphinx,* a newspaper, and was told that it was in Tahrir Square.

The paper was located in a large white building. A fountain gurgled in the quadrangle. It reminded him of a villa belonging to a rich Greek in Alexandria, one of his mother's friends. He walked through the main door and was surprised by a woman beckoning to him. But he soon realized that she was calling a messenger boy who was standing behind him. The boy gave her a parcel and went through another door, leaving him standing in front of her. Slim and elegant. A dark face and deep blue eyes that attracted him. She radiated warmth and confidence. He greeted her and asked for the advertising department. She answered in a pleasant, warm voice, "Come with me, I'm going there myself."

He followed her with mixed feelings of admiration, desire, and respect. They entered the advertising office and she pointed to a man sitting at one of the desks. A plaque bore his name, Ihsan el-Tantawi.

"I'm looking for a Sayed el-Reheimy."

"The cardiologist?"

He shook his head, expecting him to recite a long list of persons bearing that name. But he didn't.

"I don't know anyone except Reheimy the cardiologist, but don't you know anything about him? What he does, or where he lives?"

"Not at all. Only that he is a man of means. But I found only the doctor in the telephone directory."

"He might have an unlisted number, or perhaps he lives in the suburbs. In any case, an advertisement is the best means of finding him."

"Please make it a small advertisement. Let it run daily for one week. Ask them to contact me at the Cairo Hotel by telephone or mail."

"We must mention your name in the advertisement."

He thought for a moment. "Saber Sayed."

The man started filing the advertisement. Saber noticed that the girl had been following their conversation. No doubt the advertisement had aroused her curiosity. Her colleagues in the office called her Elham.

"Do you wish to state the purpose of the advertisement?" asked Tantawi.

"No." After a brief moment he added, "I imagined that he would have a large number of acquaintances, but it seems that no one knows him."

"Yours is a strange case indeed," said Tantawi. "How can you be sure that whoever contacts you is not an impostor?"

"I've got evidence."

Curiosity got the better of Elham. "This is really mysterious. Just like a movie."

Saber smiled, delighted that she was taking an interest. "I wish it could be solved as easily as in the movies."

"At least you know that he is a man of means. How did you know that?"

Saber was silent. Tantawi interjected sharply, "This sounds like an interrogation."

What a charming girl. Perhaps she would take to him. She is a pleasant breeze compared with the roaring flame at the hotel. "Miss Elham, I'm a stranger in your city."

"A stranger."

"Yes, I've just arrived from Alexandria, and I must find this man. Now that I've seen you, I feel optimistic."

She smiled, a warm, confident smile. He remembered the wine he used to drink in the Taverna with the soft strains of a violin in the background.

CHAPTER FOUR

He left the newspaper at the same time the employees departed. Thinking that perhaps he might get another glimpse of Elham, he stood for a while at the bus stop. The advertisement would take over his search for the moment. A cool breeze was blowing gently; he saw her chatting casually with a group of young people in front of the building. She took her leave from her friends and crossed into a side street and into a small cafeteria called Votre Coin. He followed her without hesitating, and seeing her sitting alone at a table, he walked in and made for the counter. He stopped at her table.

"What a pleasant coincidence! May I join you?"

"Please do," she said without undue enthusiasm. The waiter had just brought her sandwiches and an orange juice. He ordered the same.

"I hope that I'm not a nuisance. But this is usually the way with strangers."

"I welcome strangers."

"Thank you. What I meant is that strangers are always overly keen to strike up friendships. It sometimes puts people off."

"No. Not at all. You've done nothing to put me off."

"Perhaps you are going to the cinema?" he asked, taking a bite of his sandwich.

"No. We go back to work in a couple of hours. I live at the end of Giza, and you know what public transportation is like. I prefer to take my lunch here."

"Do you spend your entire lunch hour here?"

"Sometimes I go for a walk along the Nile."

They ate in silence, Saber stealing a glance whenever she wasn't looking. Her blue eyes contrasted startlingly with her dark attractive features, altogether a very pretty sight.

"What do you think of the advertisement?" he asked, "Do you think it will achieve its purpose?"

"It always does," she replied.

He was trying to arouse her curiosity, but she failed to rise to the bait. "The result is very important to me."

"Don't you really know anything about the man you're looking for?"

"I've got a photograph and some hazy information." Then, after a moment's thought: "My father has sent me to look for him. He knew him many years ago." He saw a questioning look in her eyes. "An old acquaintance," he added, smiling. "They had dealings together many years ago."

"Financial?"

"That as well."

You are trying to achieve the impossible. This girl is the type that can arouse passions. "I've never felt like this before," he said, changing the subject. She raised her eyebrows with a cynical look. "I mean, being a stranger, living on a hope, and of course, your charming presence," he explained quickly.

"I've heard that before."

"At work?"

"That's one example."

"Are you satisfied with your work?"

"Huh?"

"Would you give it up and keep house?"

"I consider this my career, not just a temporary stopgap."

His ideas of the opposite sex were firmly entrenched. They were beautiful, savage beings looking for love and passion, without principles or scruples. His mother and her circle of friends reinforced this idea. However, he did not undress her in his mind, as he usually did with any member of the opposite sex. There was something more to this girl. A certain mystery, a certain magic. Some secret he had never come across before. He would not be able to enjoy her as he had others, savagely, passionately, with an animal lust. She was unique. Something quite new to him.

"But look at the care you take over your fingernails, for example."

Indignation showed on her face, and she said sharply, "What about the care you take over your hair!"

"Please excuse me," he said hastily. "I was merely expressing my admiration." And somewhat apologetically, he added, "When I return to Alexandria I shall take back the sweetest memories of our meeting."

"Why didn't you advertise in Alexandria?"

"Well, advertising is only part of my search." He was about to settle both their bills, but she objected strongly. "If you had offered, I wouldn't have objected," he said, laughing.

He noticed that she was looking at his reflection in the mirror on the left-hand wall. A feeling of satisfaction swept over him. Perhaps he had made the same impression on her as he had made on other women. They stood up, shook hands, and separated. He fought the strong desire to follow her. When he returned to the hotel, he notified Mr. Khalil Abul Naga and Mohamed el-Sawi that he was expecting a phone call from a Sayed Sayed el-Reheimy.

"Then you are searching for your father?" said the old man, Khalil. "How did you lose him?"

"The same way that he lost me. And here I am looking for him."

"What a strange story," said the old man.

"There's nothing strange about it," he said, annoyed at the questions. "Please call me if there is a phone call."

A young man in search of his father, that's what they'll say about him. He picked up a newspaper and sat in the lounge. The telephone rang. Sayed Reheimy, hairdresser from Bulaq, Reheimy the schoolteacher, the tram driver, the grocer. Where is Sayed Sayed el-Reheimy? Why doesn't he contact him like the others? If he's dead, where is his next of kin? His funds were being rapidly depleted. The other hotel guests sat around smoking, drinking coffee, chatting. No one noticed him. Thank God. They didn't read the advertisements. Your money will run out. Where is your father? You are nothing but a pimp and a hustler. Life was beautiful when your mother was alive. Money, pleasure, more money, more pleasure. Fighting for your mother's name, in vain perhaps. But nevertheless fighting. Money, pleasure, and bloody battles.

"Cotton . . . Everything now depends on cotton," said one of the guests as he looked up from the paper at his companion.

"But this impending war? Won't it guarantee our cotton?" asked his companion.

"It won't be like previous wars."

"That's true. Nothing will remain."

"And where is God? The Creator and Protector of all this?" That's true. Where was God? He knew of the name. But that was about all. He lived in a world without religion. The telephone vigil continued. Thoughts of Elham and Khalil's wife flashed through his mind. The breeze and the flame. We need both. If my father doesn't put in an appearance, it's back to fear, hunger, and a tainted past filled with crime and sin.

The telephone rang. It wasn't for him. But as he looked toward the phone booth, he saw her. His heart stopped beating and his breathing became heavy. So she's back. That look again. A conspiracy of desire and mockery. Reheimy and Elham were soon forgotten. He left the lounge and went up to his room on the third floor. Footsteps were approaching. He opened the door. "Welcome back."

She nodded, smiling.

"We really missed you."

She laughed quietly and hurried up to the fourth floor.

"Alexandria," he said suddenly, summoning up his courage. She stopped. "Alexandria?"

"Yes."

"I don't understand."

"If you've forgotten, I can't."

"You're mad."

That sapped his newfound courage. "But aren't . . . ?"

"Don't try these old tricks on me," she interrupted and continued up the stairs.

"Well, anyway, please accept my unbounded admiration!"

She disappeared up the stairs. He leaned on the banister to get his breath and allow the fires of desire to die down. The night of the chase reappeared vividly in his imagination. Aly Seriakous, the porter, was coming down the stairs.

"I think I hear someone calling you," Saber told him slyly.

"Maybe it was Madam."

"Madam?"

"Mr. Khalil's wife."

"No. I don't think so. It might be the guest in room fifteen. I've just seen Madam enter her flat."

"Ah. Maybe. Does Madam live in the flat?"

"Mr. Khalil's flat. On the roof."

"Where was she these past few days?"

"At her mother's. She goes there every month."

He saw Khalil coming down the stairs. Hatred and resentment suddenly filled him. Beauty and the beast! He couldn't bear
the idea of staying one minute longer in the hotel. The sun and
fresh wind lifted his feelings of depression, anger, and envy.
How he wished he had more time to go sightseeing. The advertisement would not be published after tomorrow.

"Anything new?" asked Elham as he walked into her office
at the paper.

"Telephone calls and meetings, all to no avail."

"Patience."

He watched her fingers skip over the keys of the typewriter.
A sudden feeling of sadness came over him in spite of the happiness at seeing her.

Ihsan Tantawi was busy writing an obituary. He remembered
the last night in his mother's life. All his happiness and future
were now hanging on a fine thread lost in an enveloping fog.
Tantawi finished writing and looked up. "A renewal?" he asked,
smiling.

"I've seen many people, but not him," said Saber with despair
in his voice.

"Such an advertisement requires patience," said Tantawi en-
couragingly.

"But he is supposed to be very well known."

"You only know his name. All the rest is hearsay. I've lived
in many districts over the past thirty years, and I've never heard
of him."

"But I trust the person who sent me to look for him."

"Then there must be a secret which only time will reveal."

"I've got a photograph of him. It was taken thirty years ago."

"We can put it in the advertisement; it will help."

He showed him the photograph.

"He certainly looks impressive," murmured Tantawi.

Saber waited for Tantawi to comment on the resemblance. He didn't, and proceeded to discuss the costs of the new advertisement, to which Saber reluctantly agreed. His money was dwindling, and dwindling fast. He walked into the cafeteria and sat at Elham's table, waiting for her. She walked in, saw him, hesitated for a moment, then sat at his table. He ordered lunch for two.

"I've seen the photograph," she said.

"Really?"

"The resemblance is striking."

"You mean the man?"

She nodded, looking at him searchingly.

"He's my brother," he lied.

"Your brother! Why didn't you say so before?"

He smiled, but did not answer.

"Who is the beautiful woman in the photograph?"

"His late wife."

"Oh. And, your brother ... I mean how ... ?"

"He disappeared before I was born. It was the usual chain of events. A quarrel, then disappearance. And now thirty years later, my father sent me to look for him."

"What a strange story. But what makes you think he is a well-known personality?"

"My father told me. Maybe it's mere supposition. But what strikes me as strange is that Mr. Tantawi didn't notice the resemblance. Did he mention anything after I left?"

"No. But Tantawi's head is full of figures and statistics."

The waiter brought their lunch. They started eating. He stopped and said apologetically, "I'm sorry to be intruding on you like this, but I'm a lonely stranger in a big city."

She smiled at him. "How do you spend your spare time?"

"Waiting."

"How boring. But searching doesn't entail waiting."

"Waiting is unavoidable."

"What do you do while waiting?"

"Nothing."

"Impossible!"

"Now you realize how badly I need a friend," he said with a pleading look in his eyes. The sympathetic look on her face encouraged him. "You are the friend I need." She took a sip of her orange juice. "Well, what do you say?" he asked.

"You might be disappointed."

"Don't worry about that. In these matters, only the heart can tell."

"We might meet when you come in to renew the advertisement."

Laughing, he said, "In that case, you want me to keep renewing the advertisement indefinitely."

"If you are so keen on finding him."

"I am. But if the advertisement doesn't find him, I must."

She raised her glass; he raised his. "Cheers."

"I think I'd better tread carefully with you," she said with a smile.

They drank, exchanging glances and smiles. He wouldn't have chased her that night long ago had she been the other girl, the seaside girl with the salty taste and carnations in her hair. She was very dear to him. He was in love with her.

You ask who the beautiful girl is in the photograph. You didn't see her on her last night on earth. Her body wrapped in the white shroud, wasted and worn out. Suddenly he looked up and said, "I'm truly grateful!"

She recognized the trap but did not object. A happy silence reigned. The seeds were sown. The search is long and arduous and requires an occasional rest in the shade.

CHAPTER FIVE

Sore eyes from looking, searching, scrutinizing the teeming Cairo streets. The autumn clouds sailing from Alexandria are dispersed long before arriving in Cairo. But the memories of his hometown linger on. The hotel lounge has now become a torture chamber since her return. How often you've watched her sitting next to the old man, her husband. Her eyes sparkling with promise and desire. How many times did you attempt, but in vain.

Elham was lost in a dark corner of his mind, enveloped in his all-consuming fire of desire for this woman. The lounge atmosphere, cigarettes, coffee, small talk, would occasionally draw him away from his madly passionate thoughts. Maybe these people are also searching for a hope. Lost in thought, he was abruptly aroused by the doorman, Mohamed el-Sawi. "Mr. Saber . . . telephone."

At last! Was it?

"Hello?"

"Are you the person mentioned in the advertisement?"

Breathlessly, he answered, "Yes, who's calling? Sayed Sayed el-Reheimy?"

"Yes."

"Is it your photograph?"

"Yes."

He was finding it increasingly difficult to breathe. "Where can I meet you?" he almost whispered.

"Why are you looking for me?"

"Let's wait until we meet."

"Just give me an idea."

"I can't over the telephone. There's no harm in waiting till we meet."

"Can you at least tell me who you are?"

"My name is in the advertisement."

"What do you do?"

"Nothing; I've got private means."

"Why do you want me?"

"I'll tell you when we meet, anytime, at your convenience."

A brief silence at the other end. "Come now. Villa fourteen, Telbana Street in Shubra."

No one in the hotel had heard of the street. "Go to Shubra and inquire," suggested Mohamed el-Sawi.

He went to Shubra. No Telbana Street. It didn't exist. It never had. Perhaps he had heard wrong. Perhaps he was being fooled. The woman, sitting next to her husband, added to his dark mood, driving him almost to a bloodthirsty passion.

Someone had rung several times in his absence. Hope surged again.

"Were you successful?" asked Mr. Khalil.

"Almost," he replied, trying to sound cheerful. He walked to the lounge, glancing quickly at the woman. The lights had just been switched on, adding a gloomy touch to the atmosphere, which lent itself to his mood. The telephone rang.

"Hello?"

"Saber? I waited all day," the voice said accusingly.

"I didn't find the street!"

"Did you really look for it?"

"All day! Telbana, number fourteen."

"What an ass you are." A wicked laugh, then the line went dead. The bastard! Back where I started, without hope.

He left the hotel and walked into a nearby restaurant, ordered a brandy and a fish dinner. A useless day. Might as well end it on a full stomach. He had several drinks, ignoring the cost. Just like the old days. Days of wine and roses, literally, you might say. But this city has nothing but heartache and despair to offer. Every passing hour brings nearer a frightening end. What comes after waiting and searching, searching in the dark?

He would be the laughingstock of Alexandria. His fists, the only language he used, would now be turned against him. What did he have to look forward to? A life of crime, and not hope, and inevitably punishment. The woman crept back into his thoughts; the raging fire, and Elham, the gentle breeze. But of what use was all this, before he found his father? He left the restaurant and walked through the arcaded street. Passion was the only emotion driving him after his day's failure. A mad passion, just like the night of the chase. He remembered his mother. Smoking her narghileh and ruling the desires of men. Beware how you spend, my son. Poverty is the real enemy. Love many, but never be dominated by one. Love, money, nightclubs, pleasure, women. But where is Sayed Sayed el-Reheimy?

Reheimy! . . . A cry in the wilderness. The brandy stimulated his imagination. That woman dominated his thoughts momentarily. He conjured up images of wild seduction. He returned to the hotel. It was past midnight, and everyone had retired. He lit a cigarette in his ancient room. More thoughts of the woman. Then sleep. He was awakened by a sound. Opening his eyes in the dark, he heard a gentle tapping on his door. He sat up unbelievingly. Could it be! The tapping again. He got out of bed and slowly opened the door. It was barely open when a figure rushed in, closing it again quickly.

"You."

She looked around her as though trying to recognize the surroundings. "Where am I ...? I'm sorry, I seem ..." She gathered her dressing gown around her, covering her almost visible breasts. She was smiling. He pulled her toward him savagely, with all the fury and frustration that had been building up in him. I have been waiting a hundred years ...

He pulled her toward the bed and turned the lights off. "I don't even know your name."

"Karima."*

"Very ..." he murmured.

The only sounds were those of two creatures locked in passion, longing, and lust. Love in the dark, as he'd always known it. The dream was being realized in a whirlpool of passion, occasionally, but only imperceptibly, cooled by disbelief. The smell of the sea breeze once again. Memories rushing in, but being pushed into the background by passion and lust. The roar of the sea accompanying their violent lovemaking. Deep breathing, sighs, then calm reigns.

"Light me a cigarette, please."

"I didn't think you smoked."

"Only occasionally."

The match lit up her naked body, but she quickly blew it out. The smell of phosphorus blended with that of love.

"Why have you fought me all these days?"

"I never fight. I do nothing."

"I expressed my feelings about you from the very first."

She laughed softly and said, "When I saw you ten days ago I said to myself, this is it."

Triumphantly he cried out, "Alexandria?"

"No, no. I don't mean that. I said, this is the man I've been waiting for."

---

*Karima means "generous."

"What about Alexandria?"

"What about it?"

"Really? Come off it!"

"Why should I lie to you?"

"Strange that there could be two of you. Identical."

"Let's not waste time."

"How did you manage to come to my room?"

"He took his sleeping pills. All his troubles and worries converge on him in the evening."

"You have disappointed me. I told myself if you were the girl from Alexandria, then it was a good omen for my search."

"You mean your father?"

"Yes."

"What's your real story?"

"I always thought he was dead. Then I was told otherwise. That's all there is to my story."

"Maybe you're looking for money?"

"That doesn't matter now. Promise me you'll come here every night."

"Whenever I can."

He kissed her in a passionate embrace, which inevitably led to more lovemaking.

"Whenever I feel like it," she said breathlessly when they had spent themselves.

He lay on her breast, pleasantly exhausted. "Don't deny Alexandria."

"You are obsessed by an image. Take care that your search is not just a mere fantasy."

"I wish it were. Then I could rest," he said sadly.

"You really do have worries. More than I thought."

"Yes. But now my main concern is to stay here as long as possible."

"What's to stop you?"

He thought for a while, then said, "If my money runs out before I find my father, I'll have to go back to Alexandria."

"And when would you return?"

"I must look for a job."

She caressed his hand. "No," she said gently but firmly. He suddenly became aware of the trend the conversation was taking. She asked, "Why don't you look for a job here?"

"Impossible!"

"You're very mysterious. But let me tell you that money is not a problem!"

His heart missed a beat. "You must be a millionairess."

"The hotel, the money, they're all in my name."

"And your husband? Is he merely an employee?"

"No. As long as he's alive, he runs the show."

"But that doesn't concern me!" He felt himself blushing at the sly innuendo.

"Well, let's hope you find your father. That is a much better solution."

"Yes, that's very important. But from now on my main concern will be to wait for you." He tried to embrace her, but she slipped out of bed.

"Dawn is breaking. I've got to go."

He returned to his bed. The rumpled sheets and the memory of her embrace were evidence that it had all happened.

He felt that now he could do without his father. The telephone rang.

"Hello?"

A serious voice said, "Is this Saber Sayed of the advertisement?"

"Yes, yes."

"I am Sayed Sayed el-Reheimy. What do you want?"

"I must meet you."

"I am waiting for you at the Votre Coin café near the newspaper."

"I'll be there in a few minutes."

Looking around the café, he saw a man sitting at the table usually occupied by Elham. Without a doubt, it was he. He hadn't changed in thirty years. Some white hairs and a few lines on his face. Nothing more. He moved toward him, and a new fear gripped him.

The man felt him approach and stood up. "Mr. Saber?"

"Yes. And you are the man in the photograph!"

The man sat down. "You are a very young man; I have a feeling that I've seen you somewhere before. Where? I wonder."

"I'm from Alexandria and am staying at the Cairo Hotel. All day I walk the streets. I've come here several times, at this very table."

"Maybe I saw you on one of the streets. I, too, go to Alexandria occasionally. I also come here from time to time."

"When did you see the advertisement?"

"The very first day."

"Really! Well, why didn't you contact me?"

"Your advertisement indicated that you had failed to find me by other means. But I'm well known, and it's not difficult to find me. I decided to contact you when I noticed your persistent advertising."

"But that's very strange. No one I met had ever heard of you."

"Never mind about that now. Tell me what it is you want."

"I want you! But don't you notice anything?" Saber looked intently into the man's face, hoping to find a glimmer of recognition.

There was no sign of it on the man's face. "Look at my face," he said, almost shouting.

"What's wrong with it?" asked the man.

Suddenly a soft voice called out, "Saber!"

He turned to find Elham. He got up to introduce her to his father, when suddenly, to his surprise, the man rose and said, "Elham. How are you?"

To his utter amazement the girl kissed the man's forehead. "You know him!"

The man looked astonished. "When did you meet my daughter?"

"Your daughter! Oh my God!"

Before anyone could stop her, Elham rushed out of the café. Reheimy sat down and in his calm voice said, "Now tell me what it is you want."

Shaking, Saber sat down. Automatically, he took out the photograph, his birth certificate, and the marriage certificate. The man looked at each document calmly, placed them in a neat pile on the table, and just as calmly tore them to pieces. Saber jumped up and grabbed the man by his jacket, screaming, "You are denying my existence!"

"Get away from me! Don't ever let me see your face again! You're a good-for-nothing, just like your mother. I've got nothing to do with you!" He pushed him violently; Saber staggered back, fell, and banged his head on the lunch counter.

He woke up in a cold sweat, breathing heavily. He was in his hotel room, naked under the bedclothes. The sun was seeping through the shuttered window. The search; was it a dreamlike hope? A fantasy, as Karima suggested? He would have many more dreams like this one.

CHAPTER SIX

Every night the dreams haunt him. He wakes up tired and depressed, a silence continuously surrounding him. A deepening, gravelike silence. Similar to a wave before it rolls and breaks. What then? Another wave follows. His father appears in every dream. But the search is no longer the main aim of his life. Rather, it is the snatched moments of love. Love in the dark, savage, passionate with an animal desire. Darkness brings back the memories of his early youth when he was almost fatally ill.

He had panicked when he met death face to face. It was this panic that became his driving force, that drove him to a life of violence; swimming, maybe drowning, in a sea of sin, lust, and pleasure, continuously having to use his fists to defend his mother's fictitious honor.

He went to the newspaper offices and was greeted by Elham's calm smile. How refreshing she looks. A rock in his stormy sea.

"Any news?" she asked.

"I've come to renew the advertisement even though I doubt it will be of much use."

"Have you thought of any other method?"

He smiled. Little did she know that the search was now of secondary importance in his life.

"We've got a surprise for you," said Tantawi.

He sat down, his curiosity aroused.

"A woman inquired about you."

"A woman?"

"She asked about the advertisement."

"Who was she?"

"She didn't say anything; she just asked about the advertisement."

"Maybe she knows of him. Reheimy, I mean," Saber said hopefully.

"Maybe, and maybe ..."

"What's the other maybe?"

"She might know you."

"Or maybe someone's playing a trick. It's happened before," he said bitterly. Could she be his wife? His widow? Maybe it was Karima, just curious. That woman was a volatile mixture of passions and emotions, cunning and destruction.

Saber and Elham sat at their usual table in the neighboring café. He remembered his strange dream.

"You don't seem as enthusiastic as before," she remarked.

If you only knew the real reason! "It's better this way," he said, "I must not raise my hopes too high."

"Yes," she agreed, "let time be your ally in this search."

"Please let me buy you lunch, at least once."

"You are the guest, not I."

They ate in silence. He noticed a thousand questions going through her mind, mirrored in her eyes. He thought of the previous night. How strange to be two people at the same time, divided between two women, one a raging fire, the other a gentle spring breeze.

"Are you taking a holiday to carry out your search?"

She's probing now. He felt slightly uncomfortable. "I'm not employed in the real sense of the word. I have private means."

"Land?"

"My father owns some property." He could see that she

wasn't convinced. "I run his properties for him. Believe me, that's harder than holding down any job." The second lie! How he hated lying to her.

"Well, as long as you've got something to do. Idleness is man's worst enemy."

"That's very true. These past two weeks have proved it. But what do you know about idleness?"

"I can imagine it. Anyway, I've read about it."

"You have to try it to really understand it," he said bitterly.

"That's true."

"It's difficult for someone your age to have experienced enough, at least the way I have."

"If you think I'm still a child, you'd better think again!"

How delightful she is. I think I love her. He mustered more courage and said, "You know everything about me. Now tell me something about yourself."

"What do I know about you?"

"You know my name, what I do, why I'm here. And also how fond I am of you."

She smiled. "Don't mix fact with fiction!"

That is the only fact, he told himself. A dark cloud hid the sun momentarily and plunged the café in a deep gloom. "Well, I know your name and job," he said.

"What more do you want to know?"

"When did you start working?"

"Three years ago, when I graduated. I'm still studying, though. Higher studies, you know."

Thank God, she doesn't ask about my qualifications. She's too tactful for that.

"You, er, live in Giza?"

"I live with my mother. Our family is in Qalyoub. My uncle

lives in Heliopolis. We also have someone missing from the family."

"Who?" he asked, surprised.

"My father," she said, trying to hide a smile.

How incredible. He remembered his dream. Lost fathers are plentiful, it seems. Maybe they're looking for the same one. "How did you lose your father?"

"Not like your brother. Don't you think I'm giving away too much?"

He looked at her reproachfully and yet curiously.

"Actually, my parents separated when I was just a baby," she continued.

"He abandoned you?"

She laughed loudly, making him aware of his mounting curiosity. "I mean, he disappeared?" he added hastily.

"He's a well-known lawyer in Assiut. Maybe you've heard of him. Amr Zayed."

He immediately relaxed.

"I thought you were going to say Sayed Sayed el-Reheimy!"

"Would you have liked to be my uncle?" she asked, laughing.

"No," he retorted firmly.

She blushed. "My mother," she continued, "insisted on keeping me. That suited my father, as he was intent on remarrying. He paid her alimony, and we moved to my grandfather's house in Cairo. He died, and we now live alone, my mother and I."

He listened carefully, but nevertheless with some skepticism. He always doubted women and especially mothers. Elham obviously had never heard of his kind of life. Whores, pimps, bastards, and many other choice varieties. Could he give her such details as she had done? Clouds of despair and gloom hung over him. Elham was still talking. "One day my uncle said that

I should meet my father. My mother was furious. He doesn't deserve it, she argued, he never once asked about you. But my uncle insisted, saying that I was growing day by day, and I would definitely need a father."

He murmured unthinkingly, "Freedom, honor, and peace of mind."

She shrugged her shoulders and said, "My mother insisted on my not seeing him. I agreed with her point of view, that my job was more important than a father, at least more permanent. She was frightened lest he should decide to take me away from her."

Oh, just listen to her talk, that delightful child. What job or career could possibly replace freedom, honor, and peace of mind?

"I continued my studies and applied for this job, and now I'm pursuing my higher studies at night school."

"Don't you ever think of your father?" he asked.

"No. To me, he does not exist. That was his choice."

"Because you don't need him?"

"No. I don't need my mother either, but I love her and can't imagine my world without her."

You are obviously not on the brink of despair, my girl. You don't thirst for freedom, honor, and peace of mind. You are not threatened by a tainted past that could become your future overnight.

"I'm happy in my job even though I haven't got private means like you." She hit him where it hurt, unintentionally of course. How he wished he could tell her all. But he did not dare. Loneliness enveloped him when she left him to go back to the office. Despite her charm and gentleness, she aroused the animal instincts in him. He imagined her shock and horror at seduction and his ensuing shame and defeat. But to him seduction was a natural instinct, one could even say a hallowed tradition. That was his defense mechanism. To destroy every possible virtue. Elham was a shining beacon in his life but also a threat to his ego. She shook the world he was accustomed to. He could only forget his torture in Karima's fire. The beacon lighting the other half of his newfound dual life.

He walked out into the nippy November evening and strolled back to the hotel. The newly familiar sight greeted him: Khalil bent over his desk and Mohamed el-Sawi by the door.

He sat in the lounge for about an hour, smoking and scanning the papers.

He got up, went to the telephone, and dialed. "Elham, will you meet me tomorrow in the café?"

"With pleasure. Is anything wrong?"

"No, no, not at all. I want to see you whenever I can."

CHAPTER SEVEN

The nights he spends in passion with Karima. The sound of breathing echoes the rhythm and savagery of the jungle. He forgets himself then. Transcends this earth and universe, far above all fears and worries. Karima offers the pleasures and pains of a heavy meal, in contrast to the loneliness left by Elham every time they part.

Karima's nocturnal visits were uninterrupted since that first night when her gentle knock awakened him from his drunken sleep. Her influence dominating him, leaving no way for escape from these moments of passion. He pretending to be the dominant partner but fooling neither himself nor her. Never had a woman dominated him like this before. And yet he always doubted everything she said.

"I can't live without you," she whispered one night as she lay in his arms. How familiar were those words! He'd heard them in all the nightclubs and whorehouses that had been his life in Alexandria. He fought against the tide of her passion and influence. In vain. She was everything to him. Love, the hope that sent him searching for his lost father. On other evenings, she would just lie silent and still, submitting quietly and without much passion or concern. Then he would cry out in his mind for Elham, the fresh breeze to cool him in his hell with Karima. Yet it was a hell he could not live without.

How simple it had been that night on the beach by the fishing boats. You are still stubbornly attached to a memory that has long disappeared without a trace, like the waves. Karima represents not only love but also a magic potion that alleviates the agonies of this fruitless search and the whirlpool of anxieties stirred by Elham.

"You're not yourself," he said one night.

"Do you sometimes find me different?" she asked with the naïveté of a child. The cunning devil. Had she forgotten her passionate confessions of love for him? He remembered his mother on one occasion. A man had come to "visit" her, and she had thrown him out furiously; then, when he left, she had broken down, hysterically weeping. Such was the way of women.

Casually he said, "I thought you were not feeling well."

"I'm fine," she said simply. And he detected a challenge in her voice.

"I'm glad."

She caressed his cheek, saying softly, "Don't you see that you mean everything to me?"

Meaningless words. "You are everything to me as well, and more," he said slyly, "and that explains my sadness at my impending departure."

"You are talking of leaving?"

"Not talking about it doesn't mean it won't happen."

"We'll postpone it as long as possible. Unfortunately, the money instinct is strongly ingrained in men."

"There's no other solution."

"He can help when necessary."

"Is he careful about financial matters?"

"Very. He doesn't care about money so much as how it's spent."

"Is he jealous?"

"Beyond belief. We've come to an arrangement about this matter. I must keep to my bargain or I lose everything. But you, what about you? Have you nothing to do but wait for a phone call?"

"A phone call could solve everything."

"My father never meant much to me."

"Well, mine means everything."

"How did you lose him?"

"It's ancient history. I'll tell you about it one day."

"Why doesn't he contact you?"

That's the question. The cause of his torture. So many possibilities. What will happen to you if you don't find him? Disaster, calamity, a life without hope, him, or work.

"How did you manage before?" she asked, interrupting his thoughts.

"I owned thousands, once; now only tens remain."

"What work did you do?"

"No work."

"Why don't you look for work?"

"Any work I do must come through my father. It's worthless otherwise."

"I don't understand."

"Believe me."

"Go into business."

"No capital or experience."

"A job?"

"No qualifications." Then, after a pause, he said bitterly, "I'm not fit for any job."

"Only love," she whispered, running her fingers through his hair.

He smiled. "I wonder what the future holds in store for us."

"Matters are complicated, and I can't depend on my husband."

"But he's so old!"

"That's very true. I think that death has passed him by without taking too much notice of him."

"Anyway, he'll live longer than my money will last."

"And he might smell a rat, and we'd never meet again."

He pulled her closer to him. "We'll run away when all hope has gone," he whispered fiercely.

"I'm ready. But what'll we do then?"

"Hmm ... Even our love is worthless without my father."

"Be practical and stop dreaming."

"Does that mean that we must wait?"

"How can we bear waiting? And after we wait, then what?"

"Death." He sounded ominous.

"I sometimes think that he'll bury me. He's as healthy as anything. And me, I've got trouble with my liver and kidneys."

"How ironic." He laughed bitterly.

"He's a crafty old devil. At the first suspicion, I'll stop seeing you."

"I'll go mad," he almost screamed.

"So will I. But what can we do?"

"Waiting is useless, escaping futile, the telephone call, a dream; what's to be done?"

"Yes. What's to be done?"

"I think escape is the only way out."

"Never," she said breathlessly.

"Then waiting."

"Not that either," she said, almost urging him to utter some hidden thought.

"Then what?"

"Oh. Well," she said resignedly, "if we are unable to do anything, we'd better stop seeing each other."

He put his hand firmly on her mouth. "I'd rather die," he said.

"Death," she sighed. Then, as though speaking to herself, she repeated, "Yes, death."

He felt his heart beating faster, and his heavy breathing was deafening in the ensuing silence. "Why are you silent?"

"I'm tired," she answered. "Enough questions."

"But we're back where we started."

"Let it be."

"But there must be a solution," he almost pleaded.

"What?"

"I'm asking you."

"And I'm asking you."

"I was expecting a suggestion from you, a word, anything."

"No. I've no suggestions. It's a dream. Just like your telephone call. If I could inherit the money and the hotel, we'd live together forever."

He sighed. She continued: "The trouble is that we dream whenever we fail to find a way out, an escape. Dreams are our only escape."

"But the dream may be realized."

"How?"

"All by itself."

"You don't believe that, do you?"

"No!"

"And now dawn is breaking, and we've said all that can be said," she muttered.

He watched her shadow dressing in the dark. One last passionate embrace, and she left. Alone in the dark once again. Darkness like death and the grave. Your mother's grave. Alone with just your thoughts. Alone, cold, dark. In court, when sentence was passed, she cried out, "I know the monster who is behind this. I'll kill him." But her term in jail killed her, slowly but surely.

Oh, if only I could tell everything to Elham. How much easier things would be. She told me everything. I told her nothing but lies. Oh, Father, why do you insist on remaining lost?

Your mother thought she killed me. But it is I who killed her.

Then you are a criminal, a murderer; but I'll find you.

The seduction of Elham. The bloody struggle. Her screams, I'll kill you! Her torn dress revealing a naked, ravished body.

The muezzin calling the dawn prayer. Another sleepless night? But no, there was the dream, his mother, his father, and the seduction of Elham.

He got up at seven, opened the window, and heard the beggar down in the square chanting his nonsensical rhymes. O! One with the beautiful face, Christians and Jews have embraced your faith. He saw Khalil being helped down the stairs by the porter, Aly Seriakous.

He sat in the lounge watching the old man. His trembling hand, adding up the money in his ledger. The money. Oh, if only you'd drop dead, old man. What possible joy can life offer you now? Karima's beauty wasted on your sterile love. The only pleasure you get is watching her undress and having her rub your back so as to get you to sleep. Either you die or my father appears. He remembered his days of violence. That evening in one of the dingy cabarets. He almost killed a police officer in a fight.

"Don't ever get involved in a fight again," his mother had said. "I can't bear the thought of losing you. If anyone gives you trouble, just tell me. I have means of sending him to the grave." That's true; she had once dispatched one of her competitors. One of her men had taken care of her and then escaped to Libya. Everyone said Basima Omran had killed her. But there was no evidence. As for you, Khalil, death won't really make much difference to you!

CHAPTER EIGHT

"I don't think continuing with the advertisement is much use," said Saber to Tantawi the next morning. Tantawi agreed. "He must have seen the ad by now," continued Saber.

"Yes, that's almost certain," said Tantawi.

Elham joined the conversation. "Then he is refusing to make an appearance."

"Maybe he is out of the country," said Saber. "In any case, there's no sense running the advertisement any longer."

Elham's enthusiasm was mounting. "It really all depends on him now. Time is the only thing we can rely on. He'll return when he wants to. We read of many similar cases."

Little does she know that he needs his father far more than his father needs him. He needs him not only for his future but out of fear of his own dark, tainted past. A life of crime. What will happen when his money runs out anytime now? There's no one he can turn to. The only thing driving him on is his fear of a return to the past. To stop his search will mean a plunge back into a life of crime.

These dark thoughts led him to say resignedly. "Well, let's renew the advertisement."

He waited for her in the café. Their daily meeting became a sacred ritual, one to be looked forward to with eager anticipation. Then the nights of lovemaking with Karima, forgetting the calm, tender moments with Elham, only to remember them again at daybreak. A pendulum like life, swinging between animal lust and tender love, neither one overshadowing the other.

He feels attracted to and repelled by both. Each has a strong hold over him, arousing a feeling of protest within him. And yet he can't give either up. The choice can never be made. El-ham representing clear, cloudless skies, Karima thunder and rain, but also like the Alexandria skies. Beloved Alexandria. The nights he spent at home in Alexandria, drinking beneath a cloudy sky, warming himself with creatures of lust and desire. Why does she deny that she hails from his past? She who is reminiscent of those wild nights made spicy by the salty air, wild like the stormy sea. She who is so much like him, hot-blooded, passionate, angry. Elham, so much the opposite, re-mote on a hill, out of reach.

She remarked on his silence, so he said heavily, "When this search is over, one way or the other, there'll no longer be any reason for me to stay."

She cast her eyes to the floor and said, "Have you decided when you're leaving?"

"I can't bear the thought of life away from Cairo."

"A lovely thought. I hope you realize it," she said earnestly, looking straight at him.

"I think of nothing else."

"But what about your family and your work?"

"There is always a way. Sometimes I think . . ." He was silent for a moment, then continued: "Sometimes I think that I didn't come here to look for Sayed Sayed el-Reheimy at all, but rather to find you. We sometimes go chasing something, and during the chase we come across the thing we are really looking for."

A look of tenderness and warmth crept into her eyes, and she said seriously, "In that case, I'm heavily indebted to Sayed Sayed el-Reheimy."

The dam burst. "Elham, I love you. My love has been grow-ing ever since I met you. You mean everything to me, the very reason for my existence. I've never felt like this before. Every word I'm saying I mean from the very bottom of my heart."

Her lips moved silently.

"Isn't it so with you?" he asked, urging her out of her silence.

"Yes, and more," she said quietly.

He touched her hand and stroked it gently. Every fiber in him was singing; then he remembered Karima and their forthcoming meeting in a few hours. Clouds suddenly darkened his mood. He had loved more than one woman before, but now when he was with Karima, Elham pulled him, and vice versa. If only he could make them one person, one soul, one body!

"Have you ever been in love before?" he asked, trying to blot out his thoughts.

"No, never. Childhood romances maybe. I was once in love with a film star who is long since dead. No, Saber, I have never loved before. I was engaged once, but we broke up when he asked me to leave my job. My colleagues at work, they make their passes, that's inevitable. I'll tell you all about that later, if you promise that you won't leave; well, at least not forget Cairo."

"If I go to the ends of the earth, I'll never forget Cairo."

"That's good to hear. Now tell me what you know about love."

"I never knew it could be like this."

"I know a little about life, and I feel that when I look into your eyes I see a person of great goodness."

He quickly hid his surprise. "What do you mean?"

"I don't know. Please don't ask me to explain. You, you, it's something in the look in your eyes. It's reassuring, confident."

Oh. These beautiful, blue, unseeing eyes. Me, a good person? What about the old days? Where have the wild nights gone?

Have they vanished without a trace? Oh, Father, please come and save me from my predicament.

"I don't want to praise myself, but my love for you, Elham, proves to me that I'm a better person than I thought I was," he said, half believing himself.

"You're better than that. Look at the relentless way you are looking for your brother. Did you ever know him?"

"No."

"And yet you are searching for him as though you knew him all your life. This alone proves to me what a noble person you are."

Damn! All my lying. Elham's words are as empty as a silence.

"I've only been asked to look for him, just like any other task."

"No. Even if you find him, that won't be to your advantage, at least materially; don't deny your good qualities."

Karima, like him, had been rubbed in the dirt for a long time. They had that in common. They could communicate, even at a distance. At the climax of their lovemaking she would whisper, "When will the obstacle to our love vanish?" That would fill him with fear, a fear compounded in the dark love nest, a darkness that could easily lead to crime.

Karima wouldn't imagine that he could kill just to avenge another woman. Yet he had done so before. He had blood on his hands; it was not a new experience for him.

The old man's clinging to life had no meaning except to drive him to an inevitable end. Elham, you have fallen in love with a criminal. I'll go mad if I continue lying to you.

The thought of murder fills your mind. You've done it before. Confess . . . Confess that you are worthless and poor, and that Reheimy is your father, not your brother. Confess that without him you are not worth a fistful of dust. Confess your past. She'll scream with fright and pain. The light in her eyes will go out. Then she'll discover the truth. If your mother had brought you up properly, you would have been a successful pimp by now. But no ... she protected you in her golden cage, and now you suffer eternal torture. She resurrected your father and thus took away from you the comforts of despair and hopelessness.

"My mother thinks you should start a business in Cairo. She knows a lot about you," said Elham, interrupting his thoughts.

Mother! He feared mothers. Like his mother, she might find out the truth. She wouldn't be fooled by the look in his eyes.

"What kind of business?"

"That depends on what you can do."

Drinking, dancing, fighting, and lovemaking.

"Real estate management is the only thing I know."

"I don't know anything about your schooling."

He remembered that transient phase in his life. His brief sojourns in Arabic and foreign schools.

"My father didn't give me the chance to finish my education. He needed me to help him, especially when he fell ill."

"Think of some business. I've got some friends who can help you."

"All right. But I must first consult my father."

They got up to leave. "I wish I could kiss you, Elham, but it's impossible here."

His senses all screamed out: Leave Elham. She's like your father, full of promise but only a dream. Karima is just an extension of your mother. She represents pleasure and crime. Go back to Alexandria. Pimp for your enemies. Kill. Take Karima; take her money. Draw Reheimy out of the darkness. Marry Elham. Cairo winters are cruel. Streets are crowded, a marketplace of humanity. There you are lost in a fruitless search. You can have any woman you choose, offering a life of pleasure and no worries. But instead you choose Reheimy. Maybe he's just a charlatan who convinced your mother he was somebody.

You must have seen your father a thousand times every day while scanning the countless faces in the Cairo streets. He rejects you, or perhaps fears you. Maybe he's dead? Winter speeds up the darkness. It springs upon you suddenly and closes over you like the waves, drawing you in.

The porter of the hotel had told him of a soothsayer; perhaps he might help. He had gone to him, only to find that he had been arrested as a humbug. Since when was that a crime? The hotel became his prison. The lounge was filled with people, smoke, and noise. The faces changed, but the conversation always remained the same. He heard a man ask, "But doesn't that mean the end of the world?"

"To hell with it," said another.

Laughter and smoke filled the room. A man asked him, "Are you for the East or the West?"

"Neither," he replied disinterestedly. Then he remembered his plight and said, "I am for war . . ."

CHAPTER NINE

Karima didn't come that night. He lay on his bed in an alcoholic stupor imagining the absent lovemaking, trying to quench his lust. It was past midnight and still no Karima. She had never missed a night in his arms before. He kept a constant vigil all night, gradually losing all hope of her turning up. The dawn prayer announced the end of his hopeless wait. He slept for a few hours and woke up at ten.

As Saber breakfasted in the lounge, he watched the old man chat with the doorman. When will he wake up and find the old man not at his desk? How was he going to ask Karima about her absence last night? A heated argument broke out between two of the residents. He watched the vigorous gesticulations and the empty threats. Intensely annoyed, he got up and walked out of the hotel.

At lunch Elham looked serious. He felt much better than he had earlier. He always did when he saw her. "Our meeting every day is the only meaningful thing in my life," he told her with happiness clearly ringing in his voice.

"I don't cease to think about us," she said, looking at him with love and tenderness in her eyes.

He felt a tightness in his chest at her innocent attempts to capture him. He felt annoyed at the nightly defeats Elham suffered at the hands of her powerful enemy. "I'm glad to hear that. Me, too, I think of nothing else."

"Tell me, then," she said coyly.

"I think of work, and marriage."

"So you're finally convinced by my suggestion?"

"Yes, but first I must finish my mission here, one way or the other; then I'll leave and make arrangements with my father." He despised himself for his lies. How he wished he could confess all, come what may. The dilemma was something totally novel to him, a constant torment. "Let's go to the cinema," he said almost desperately.

They held hands in the dark. Always in the dark. But he felt at peace and kissed her hand; the gentle, intoxicating whiff of her perfume stirred his passions. He remembered the torture that lay in store for him at night. Karima. Desperately he tried to obliterate the thoughts.

"How cruel," whispered Elham, referring to the scene from the film.

He wasn't following, so he quickly said, "One moment away from you is far more cruel."

He watched the scene unfolding on the screen. A man was abusing a girl. The dialogue to him was disjointed and meaningless. Just like watching people's lives out of context, detached, disinterested. We laugh when tears are called for and cry when we are supposed to laugh. Your search for your father, for example, must appear amusing to people reading the advertisement. Will Karima come tonight? Is it going to be another night of agony and torture? He watched Elham's face; she was following the film intently. He tried slipping his hand out of hers, but she clung tightly to it.

They walked to the bus stop; she got on, and he stood for a moment watching the bus disappear around the corner. He walked to the grocer next to the hotel, ordered a sardine and pastrami sandwich, and washed it down with half a bottle of brandy. The vigil in his room began shortly after midnight. Oh, the humiliation he suffered. Never before had he felt like this.

A hungry fear, fear of futile search, fear of fear itself. The night passed slowly and no Karima.

There she was the following afternoon. Sitting next to her husband. Just as he had seen her the first time. She avoided his long, hungry look as he sat in the lounge. She didn't know the madness of his passion, or she wouldn't provoke him so. She got up and went upstairs. As their eyes met for a moment, there was a clear warning in her glance. What does her look mean? The old man hadn't changed in his behavior toward her. He was too old to hide his emotions. Saber thought of following her, but as though she had read his thoughts, she raced up the stairs.

His money was running out. The search had become nothing more than a meaningless farce. The nights followed in the same monotonous pattern. A meal and heavy drinking. Hope by midnight. Waiting in the dark, night after night.

"Someone called you today," said the doorman one evening as Saber returned, drunk as usual. The telephone. Its ring lacked the excitement and anticipation it had had previously. But still a miracle could always occur.

"A woman's voice," continued the doorman, noticing Saber's indifference.

"Concerning the advertisement?"

"No. She just asked if you were here."

Elham. He had not seen her for a couple of days. His mood was such ... He lay in the dark. A knock on the door. He jumped up like a maniac, opened the door, and dragged her violently inside.

"You!" he almost screamed out. He pulled her savagely toward the bed, unable to contain his passion. "You, damn you, you devil!"

"You're tearing my skin," she cried.

"You tore my nerves."

"What about me! Don't you know how I felt?"

He tried to tear off her gown, but she struggled.

"No, no don't. It's dangerous. I've got to tell you something, then I must leave."

"The devil himself can't save you now," he snarled.

"Shut up! You're drunk. One false move, and you'll spoil everything."

He sat her down on the bed. "What happened?"

"When I returned to my flat the last time I was here, he was awake. I made the usual excuses for being out of the room. But I think Aly Seriakous, the porter, saw me. I'm not sure, but I'm very scared."

"You're imagining things."

"Perhaps. And perhaps not. We can't risk it. We'll lose everything. Love, hope, our future. One word from him will condemn us to eternal poverty and misery. Don't you ever forget that." She sighed heavily, then continued: "That's why I stopped coming to you. I obviously couldn't explain to you before. I imagined your torture through mine. But my husband has given me all his wealth only on the condition that I'm absolutely faithful to him. He told me I'm his hands, eyes, daughter, wife; in fact, everything. I must be true to him during his few remaining days."

"Then what are we going to do?"

"I must stop coming here."

"But this is madness!" he growled.

"This is the only sane thing to do."

"How long must I wait? Till when?"

"I don't know," she sighed.

"My money will run out, and I'll have to leave."

"I can give you some to keep you here as long as possible."

"That won't change the inevitable."

"I know. But what can we do? I'm suffering just as you are."

"My plight is worse. I'm threatened with torture and poverty."

"I'm suffering for both of us. Why can't you realize this?"

"When will the old man die?" he muttered to himself.

"Do you think I know? I'm not a clairvoyant."

"Then what are you?" he snapped.

"An unhappy woman. Unhappier than you can imagine."

"Maybe death will answer our call, and he'll die suddenly."

"Maybe."

"He's an old man; he can't live forever."

"He might die tonight or in twenty years' time. His elder sister died two years ago," she said with a sigh. Dawn, the cock crowing, the muezzin calling the faithful to prayer. "There's nothing we can do. I must go."

"I won't see you unless he dies?"

"There's nothing we can do."

"There is," he said forcefully. The silence was deafening. He continued: "We've so far spoken in riddles, in the dark. We are going to speak frankly now. I must kill him!"

Her body trembled and so did her voice. "You don't really believe what you're saying. I'm not cruel or savage. My only fault is that I love you beyond measure. We must wait."

"So that he lives as long as his sister?" he retorted with contempt.

"Or whenever the Almighty decides."

He had already decided. His blood was boiling and he felt hot despite his nakedness and the cool winter night. He paced the room furiously. "What happens after the crime?" he asked in a matter-of-fact tone of voice. She was silent. The darkness was oppressive. "Don't waste time," he snapped. "What happens after the crime?"

She gasped slightly as though choking over words, then very softly she said, "We wait a while. We can meet secretly, then I'll be yours. Me and the money."

He clenched his fists. "We have no choice. Desperation has driven us to this."

"Yes, unfortunately that's true."

"How must we set about it?" he asked.

She replied, quicker than he expected, "Study the neighboring building carefully."

So. She's got everything planned. But never mind. It's all because of her love for me.

"The apartment opposite the hotel is used as a secondhand clothing store. It's always empty at night. And it's easily accessible. The roof of the building and our roof adjoin," she continued in a hushed voice. "You can cross over to our side easily. You must wait for him in the flat."

"He comes up at about half past eight, nine?" asked Saber.

"Yes. Choose a date when I go to visit my mother. I go regularly once a month."

"Incredible that I've been here almost a month already," he said.

"You can then cross back to the other roof and leave the building without anyone noticing you."

His voice trembled slightly as he said, "We often hear of such crimes, after they are discovered."

Coldly, she replied, "But we never hear of those that are not discovered."

She was just like his mother. Utterly ruthless. "Is there anything else we haven't covered?" he asked.

"Yes. You must steal something as a motive for the crime."

"What shall I steal?"

"Leave that to me. But be sure to leave no traces."

"I'd better be careful, hadn't I?" he muttered.

"Our lives are now bound together. Should anything happen to you, it will also be my fate. We have no other choice."

He shook his head as if he couldn't believe the entire conversation. "Madness ... madness ... do you think all this will really happen?"

"Study the building carefully. Make sure no one sees you. There are a few days left before I go to my mother. You've got the guts it takes. Now let's go over it once again, step by step."

He was not listening, lost in deep, dark thoughts.

CHAPTER TEN

He breakfasted on eggs, cheese, fruit, and a glass of milk. He watched the other guests in the lounge. Look carefully at them; in a short while a vast chasm will separate you from them.

When night falls you are going to sign a bloody pact as your gateway to crime. There goes old man Khalil, facing the cold morning, his hand trembling unceasingly, not thinking of death. Your life will end at ten this evening. You don't know that, but I do. Take the advice of one who has lost hope; don't bother about trivial matters any longer. I share with God the realm of the unknown. The telephone rang. Saber laughed audibly. Was that his father ringing at the eleventh hour?

Mohamed al-Sawi answered, "No, no, you've got the wrong number."

No, no. And no to you, Sayed el-Reheimy! You've denied your son, and now your son denies you. Your son will seek freedom, honor, and peace of mind somewhere else. Don't yawn, Khalil. Soon you'll sleep forever. Why do you persist in following an inevitable destiny? Explain to me what it all means; I, your killer, will enjoy your fortune, my mother sunk to the lowest depths, my father mercilessly silent, my hopes dependent on destruction. Explain all this. What is it all about? A week has passed, and I think of nothing but the crime. How different were my dreams as the train left Alexandria. These other men, the guests, have none of them committed a crime? All this talk of money, war, luck, will it never cease? They predict the future and yet are so ignorant about what is going to happen right here under their very noses.

Saber left the hotel at ten, nodding to Khalil on his way out. *I left the hotel at ten and didn't return till one in the morning,* he kept repeating to himself. He looked at the entrance of the neighboring building. Like a teeming marketplace. People going in and out. The roof was empty, and no other overlooked it. It would get dark after five.

He thought of visiting Elham, but the idea was crowded out by his immediate thoughts. He couldn't bear to talk to her while he was contemplating blood. What was he going to tell her before he left her forever?

He passed the newspaper building, and an overwhelming sadness descended upon him. He remembered their meetings, her concern over his problem, his inability to match her love. He killed time by walking aimlessly, had lunch at the grocery in Clot Bey Street, and washed it down with a couple of brandies.

"Terrible weather," said the grocer.

"I'm a criminal descended from criminals," he cried out as he left the shop. The grocer laughed; brandy does strange things to people!

He suddenly decided that he must see Elham. She was not at the café; the waiter told him that she had left immediately after lunch. His sudden desire to see her waned. He waited until five o'clock and then walked back to the arcaded street, standing in the darkness opposite the entrance to the building adjoining the hotel. The beggar was singing loudly, as usual. He noticed the doorman of the building busy in conversation with a street vendor. He took this opportunity to cross the street and enter the building. It was crowded with people. Many eyes fell upon him, but none saw him. He looked at every face carefully, to check whether any of the hotel guests were in this building for one reason or another.

He finally reached the roof. It was light enough to see that the roof was deserted. He looked around and saw that no other building overlooked it. His eyes rested on the hotel roof. Karima was there gathering the washing from the line. The sudden sight of her shook him. She must have been waiting for him. Maybe she had even watched him cross the street and enter the building.

She beckoned to him to approach. He did; seeing her renewed his determination to carry out his task.

"Did anyone see you?" she asked, turning her back to him.

"No one."

"Aly Seriakous is downstairs. I'll wait at the top of the stairs until you cross over."

She left with the washing and disappeared around the corner. He waited a moment, looked around him, then jumped onto the hotel roof. He proceeded cautiously until he arrived at the door of the apartment.

"The door is open. Come in," she whispered.

He took a deep breath and entered, finding himself in a darkened hall. She joined him, closing the door behind her, and switched the light on. Her eyes were sparkling but her face was deathly pale. Gone were her seductive looks. They hugged, nervously and without passion, looking at each other with some bewilderment, like two frightened, lost children.

"Any slip-up and we're lost," he said.

"Get hold of yourself," she said. "No one suspects a thing. Everything will turn out the way we planned it."

She took him through the flat. The hall led into a large bedroom with an adjoining door to a smaller dining room. He glanced at the furniture in the bedroom. The large bed, the sofa, the Turkish divan, all seemed to stare at him with disinterested eyes. He was about to tell her his feelings, then thought better of it.

"What an ugly room," he said instead.

She seemed to recover from the tension of the moment. "Yes. You must hide here in the bedroom. The moment you hear the front door, get under the bed."

"Is it a wooden floor?"

"Yes, it's carpeted all over."

"He'll close the front door?"

"Yes. Sawi takes him up. Especially when I'm away. He locks the door himself and leaves the key either in the lock or on the table, here. You unlock it and leave."

"I might meet someone on the roof."

"No. Seriakous, the porter, retires after my husband comes up. His room is on the third floor."

"They'll ask how the . . ."

"The windows will be closed, so either he forgot to lock the door after Sawi left or else someone knocked and he opened the door," she said quickly.

"Is it possible that he'd open the door to someone without asking who it was?"

"Maybe he heard a familiar voice."

"Then suspicion will fall on those he knows in the hotel."

Coldly and impatiently, she answered, "They won't pin it on an innocent person. The important thing is that you get away." She pointed to her handbag. "I've taken the money and some jewelry. I opened the cupboard with a knife and threw some clothes on the floor. Did you get gloves?"

"Yes."

"Very good; here is the iron bar." She pointed to the table in the middle of the room. "Don't touch it without your gloves on, and be careful not to drop anything under the bed." Her face seemed even paler contrasted with her glittering eyes. "I must go," she said. They embraced.

"Stay for a while," he pleaded, clinging to her.

"No, I must go."

"Have you forgotten anything?"

"Pluck up your courage and act calmly, and . . ."

"What?"

She gave him a strange, distant look. "Nothing," she whispered. "Get under the bed."

They embraced a third time. She broke away quickly and left him, calling loudly for Aly Seriakous. Quickly, he hid under the bed. Karima returned with the servant and told him to close the windows. She waited until he had done so, then switched off the lights and left the room.

Saber got out from under the bed. It was pitch dark. He put on his gloves and groped toward the table and found the bar. He gripped it firmly and crossed the room and sat down on the edge of the bed. Nothing else existed at the moment. Just the feel of the bed, the smell of her perfume, and the crescendo of silence. No escape now. One death-dealing blow. One blow is better than all this endless waiting and futile searching. Karima's love, like a thin cloud and yet more dangerous than the task he was about to perform. The beggar was still chanting away. Did he ever stop? It was a lost call. Just like the advertisement, and his mother's wealth, and those days of long ago. When would he see Karima again? Embrace passionately and safely?

He heard the servant Seriakous humming softly on the roof. Then silence and darkness. After what seemed an eternity, he heard the key turn in the lock. He quickly crawled under the bed. Footsteps approached, the door opened, and the room flooded with light. He could scarcely breathe, and he thought that his heartbeats could be heard a mile away. Six feet appeared to him. The old man was saying, "You can go now, Aly, but don't forget the plumber."

Two feet disappeared. Khalil sat on the edge of the bed, his feet a mere two inches from Saber's face. "I'll meet him tomorrow. But I won't stand for any nonsense," Khalil said.

"Yes, I agree," said Sawi, the doorman.

"He's a cunning devil. He came close to death four times, and he still hasn't learned his lesson."

"You are a generous man, master." After a short silence, Sawi asked, "May I leave you now, Mr. Khalil?"

"No. Stay a while. My back is aching, and I have a terrible headache."

How long will he stay? Will he spend the night with the old man? Saber shuddered at the thought. Khalil was busy saying his prayers. How appropriate. When he had finished, he said, "Help me with my robe and shoes, Sawi." Rustling and movement then, "Get me my sleeping tablets from the drawer."

Where is that drawer?! If it was in the cupboard, the fake theft would be discovered. He held his breath in anticipation. He breathed again when he heard the old man drink water, swallowing the tablet. Then he felt Khalil lie on the bed and pull the covers around him.

"Sawi, I can't get up. Lock the door and open it at the usual time tomorrow morning. Good night."

Darkness, then the dim light of a small lamp. You will find your master a corpse tomorrow morning. How did the killer enter? How will he escape afterward? The window, the one overlooking the roof. How will they reconstruct the crime? He was going to explode with tension and fear. All these thoughts, all this planning. You must carry it out. You must. Your heartbeats are deafening. You can't think. Will he fall asleep before I explode? Snoring. Just like his mother on her last night. The death shroud, the weeping skies in Alexandria. Forget that now. He crawled out from under the bed. He stood up, gripping the bar firmly in his gloved hand.

Khalil was hidden under the bedclothes. Only his head showed slightly under the pillow. He felt better at not seeing his face. He approached with renewed courage. He raised the bar. Suddenly the old man turned restlessly. Saber stood rooted in his place, arm raised, bar above his head. The old man opened his eyes. Their eyes met. No sign of recognition in Khalil's eyes. Saber realized his plight and brought his arm crashing down. He was taken aback by the fantastic force of the blow and the sickening sound of the impact. The old man uttered one soft cry, then a whimper, then silence. The body shuddered once violently, then was still. Saber didn't bother to make sure he was dead. He rushed to the window, opened it, looked out, and jumped quickly onto the roof, closing the window behind him.

Was the iron bar soaked with blood? Was the roof deserted? What time was it? He crossed the roof. Why didn't he wash the bar in the bathroom? Should he throw it from the roof of the building? That would be idiotic. He heard voices on the stairs. He looked over the banister. The third floor was dark, but the light shone on the second floor. He wiped the bar with his left glove, then slowly went down the stairs. He came to the second floor. The light was shining from an open apartment. Three men came out and followed him down the stairs. He slowed down until they passed him. He came to the ground floor and left the building with the three men as though he were one of them. He noticed the doorman of the building sitting in his small room by the entrance. Outside he took a deep breath. Did anyone recognize him? Were his clothes bloody? He saw a taxi on the other side of the street. But he dared not cross. Someone might see him from the hotel. He turned away from the building and crossed the street, and then doubled back toward the taxi. The beggar was through for the day. He was getting up and moving toward him. He waited a few paces away from the taxi.

The beggar passed him. For the first time he got a good look at him. How repulsive. A thin, sallow face, a crooked nose, and red, bloodshot eyes. A dirty bedraggled beard and a head covered by a black patchy skullcap. What did this man have to sing about? And yet he sang all day. The beggar passed him with the expected stench that went with his appearance. He rushed toward the taxi and asked the driver to take him to the Nile, at the place where some boats were moored. Had anyone seen him leave the building? Did anyone notice the glove and the bar? Why was the taxi moving so slowly? The driver was annoying him with meaningless chatter.

"Isn't that right?"

"Huh . . ."

"I mean, instead of this madness, I tell myself, patience is a virtue." Why doesn't this idiot shut up? What is he saying anyhow? The banks of the Nile were plunged in darkness. No one would see the glove, the bar, the blood. Rowing at such an hour must surely be strange. But not strange when compared with other things.

Now you can get rid of the glove and the bar. Wash your hands carefully in the muddy Nile waters. He suddenly felt exhausted. He let the boat drift with the current. Nothing on shore was worthwhile. How pleasant it was just to drift with the tide. The eyes and their look, the cry; these could never be forgotten. The beggar's eyes, did they issue forth tears or blood? Nothing mattered now, not even the search for his supposed father. But where are you drifting?

Suddenly a piercing blast woke him from his trance. A river steamer passed within inches of him. His boat rocked violently in its wake. He took the oars and rowed back to the mooring place. The sky was pitch black. Not a star in sight. He suddenly shivered and for the first time that evening felt the winter cold. He walked along the island briskly to keep warm.

It happened while he was crossing the Kasr el-Nil bridge. A large sedan was waiting at the traffic light. A man sat at the wheel. Dignified and obviously well-to-do. That face. Was it possible? The light turned, and the car moved.

Sayed el-Reheimy! The cry rent the cold night air. He chased after the car, running like a maniac. But the car sped on and disappeared from sight. He stopped running, gasping for breath. It was him. Reheimy. After thirty years. He didn't even get the car's number. What was the use now? How could he trust his eyes if he didn't even feel the cold? His senses had deserted him. Reheimy meant nothing to him now. His only hope lay in Karima.

She must be awake now, thinking. A strong bond held them, and yet how he wished to see Elham and confess. The clock in the square showed midnight. He decided to return to the hotel. What a hateful prospect. He shuddered as he passed the building next to the hotel. He remembered the repulsive beggar and wondered where to seek refuge.

Sawi, the doorman, was sitting in Khalil's chair. He was still awake. Saber dared not enter. But to go out again might raise suspicions.

"You look exhausted," Sawi said.

"It's very cold outside," he said cautiously.

"She rang again," the doorman said, with a knowing smile.

"Who?"

"You know best."

Elham! Cowardly! Just like Reheimy.

"Your city offers nothing but problems," he said bitterly.

"Life is nothing but problems. Any news?"

He realized Sawi was asking about his search. "I'll look for him tomorrow. At the cemetery."

He nodded and went up the stairs to his room. Room number thirteen!

CHAPTER ELEVEN

He left his bed at six in the morning without having had a moment's sleep. All night haunted by dreams, dreams, and more dreams. A quarrel between him and Karima in front of the old man, who didn't seem to notice him. But if he had dreamed, then he must have fallen asleep. It's very cold. But you can take it. After all, you're a hardened criminal. He switched on the light and was shocked to see his right glove still on! He stared at it in horror. He must have gotten rid of the bar and the left glove and forgotten this one. He had gone to the riverbank, strolled around the island, chased after the car, crossed streets, waved to the doorman, and all the time he had his right glove on!

He felt a cold, creeping terror. What happened to all your careful planning? What traces have you left behind? You must check everything, the bedsheets, the blanket, the floor, your shoes, socks, jacket, shirt, handkerchief. He felt physically sick with fear and doubt. The investigating eyes will not miss a thing. He must get rid of the glove. He wrapped it in his towel, grabbed his soap, and went to the bathroom, his small scissors in his pajama pocket. He cut the glove into small pieces and flushed them down the toilet. He then washed his face and left the bathroom to return to his room, only to meet Aly Seriakous in the corridor.

"Good morning, Mr. Saber, you're up early this morning."

Damn . . . What are you doing here? . . . The guest in room thirteen was up earlier than usual, that's the only thing I noticed, Officer. That's exactly what the wretch will say. Damn!

81

Damn! This was a bad omen. Did he wipe the floor after having disposed of the glove? Curses! He's going to the bathroom. He thought he had seen what looked like bloodstains by the sink. He stood rooted to the spot, his eyes glued to the bathroom door. The porter came out of the bathroom.

"Can I do anything for you, sir?"

He ignored him and went straight for the bathroom to look for bloodstains.

"I forgot my soap," he said apologetically, trying to appear calm as he left the bathroom again. The man smiled.

"You had it in your left hand."

Catastrophe! Laughing nervously: "That's the hazard of waking early. I couldn't sleep, there was a terrible racket outside." He entered his room still laughing nervously. What a bad start. But no need to exaggerate the dangers. He inspected his clothes carefully while dressing. Looking up at the ceiling, he imagined Khalil lying on his bed. He shuddered. Murders happen every day, he reassured himself. It would be madness to leave now for Alexandria. Have I forgotten anything? Evidence could be found in the strangest places. He thought of taking his jacket to be dry-cleaned. But how would he wrap it? This would certainly draw attention to him. Probably by this afternoon he would be answering questions. The dangers of his situation weighed heavily upon him. He must leave the hotel before they discover the crime. That was more important than the jacket. He took a last look around the room. Will it betray him? Mohamed el-Sawi was performing his morning prayers as Saber walked into the lounge. There were a few people around as he sat down to his breakfast. The porter, Aly Seriakous, walked up to him.

"You forgot this, Mr. Saber."

His wallet! It must have fallen out of his jacket as he was looking through it. He opened it.

"Thank you very much, Aly," he said, giving him ten piasters.

"I found it on the floor by your bed."

How many mistakes were still undiscovered? he wondered.
This blind force driving you will soon bare you before the
whole world. You will stand naked, just as you were born. Just
as your mother delivered you into this world. Your mother, the
real killer! Khalil had snored, just as she had done on her last
night. He noticed one of the residents smiling at him, as though
he were reading his thoughts. The lounge became unbearable.
He walked out of the hotel and was greeted by the singing of
the beggar. How repulsive he looks. Maybe he's happy just
singing away all day and every day. Sawi, the doorman, going
up to the apartment on the roof. Knocking on the bedroom
door.

"Mr. Khalil! Wake up! Wake up! Mr. Khalil, it's almost eight
o'clock. Mr. Khalil! Mr. Khalil!" He pushes the door open and
looks carefully in. "Mr. Khalil," quietly. Then: "Oh my God!
Mr. Khalil! Master! Master! Help! Help! Aly! Aly! Help! Mr.
Khalil has been murdered! Police! Police! Help!"

My mother disappeared, never to be found by my father. My
father disappeared, never to be found by me. Maybe I can also
disappear. Just vanish without a trace. Then sometime, somewhere, Karima will be in my arms, the promises of a comfortable, happy, secure life finally fulfilled.

He walked, not seeing anyone, not hearing anyone. Just
walked, occasionally sitting down at a café for a brief rest. But
for him there could be no rest. He passed by the High Court
building. Dark clouds were passing overhead. Clouds, reminiscent of Alexandria.

He must see Elham. Toward the late afternoon he headed for
the café, their usual meeting place. It looked strange to him

today. Everything was strange today. He felt a sudden mad urge to confess everything. The truth! For once!

She looked at him reproachfully. "Why should I greet you if you've been avoiding me?" she said, looking at him with her deep blue eyes, pretending to be cross. She sat down, staring at him uncomprehendingly. "And you're not even talking," she continued.

"I'm sorry, Elham. I was very busy and completely exhausted."

"Not even a call on the telephone?"

"Not even. Let's not discuss this now. Let me just look at you."

They were silent. Just sitting there looking at each other. The beggar's chant ringing in his ears. Why did he insist on meeting her? Maybe their meeting was a temporary shelter from the storm that was about to break. She's smiling even though she shook my bloodied hand! He felt tears creeping into his eyes. The farewell tears.

"You look exhausted."

"I've seen him," he said quietly, almost in a whisper.

Her eyes widened. "Your brother?"

"Sayed. Sayed el-Reheimy."

"Then your mission is over?" she cried, overjoyed.

He recounted the story wearily.

"There is a possibility that it's him," she said hopefully.

"And also that it isn't," he retorted.

"When will all this be over?" she asked pleadingly.

"I consider it finished."

"You really look tired."

"I've been meeting a lot of people during the past few days."

"About your brother?"

"Yes."

They drank their juice in silence. A smile crossed her lips and she asked, "Didn't you have any time to think of me?"

"All the time."

"What did you think?"

When are you going to confess? When, when? Save yourself all these lies.

"Say something," she said, still coyly. "Last time, we spoke of a new job here in Cairo."

Confess. Confess. That's all you're thinking of. Otherwise, you'll explode.

"Yes, yes," he said hastily, "I haven't forgotten."

"In spite of your worries?"

"I've been thinking of the various aspects of the new job."

He could not resist any longer. "Elham. I love you. I love you with all my heart. I've been lying to you all this time."

"What do you mean?" she asked, bewildered.

"My love for you is what drove me to lie."

"I don't understand." Confusion covered her face.

"I told you I was searching for my brother. Well, the truth is that I'm searching for my father."

"Your father?"

"Yes, yes. My father."

"How did he disappear? Perhaps like my father?"

"No. I always believed that he was dead. But my mother, just before dying, told me that he was alive and said that I must find him."

"Well, that doesn't change anything," she said, looking him straight in the eye.

"But I'm broke," he cried. "I don't own a thing. My mother was rich, and I always led a comfortable life. But when she died all she left me was her marriage certificate and the photograph as evidence. Other than that, I'm not worth a thing."

Bewilderment and shock filled her eyes. What if he told her the whole truth about his mother?

"You look worried," he said quickly.

"No, no. Just surprised," she replied haltingly.

"I'm not worthy of you, Elham. I'll never forgive myself for deceiving you."

"I understand everything. I understand why you lied."

"What I can't bear is that I made you love someone not worthy of you."

"Your love for me, is that a lie?"

"Never. Never. I love you with all my heart."

She sighed. "It's your love for me that forced you to tell the truth, isn't it?"

"Yes, yes. That's true."

"Then you've done nothing wrong by hiding the truth."

"But I must leave you."

"Why?" she cried out, swallowing hard.

"I'm penniless; I have no one; I can't do anything."

"Money is not everything. As for having no family, what do we need family for? And besides, there are many things you can try your hand at."

"I doubt that. I've no education, no experience, I never had a job before. You see, there is no hope unless I find my father."

"And will your father be a substitute for everything else?"

"My mother told me that he was a man of considerable means."

She paused briefly, then: "But the advertisement . . . the name . . . the telephone directory . . . I mean . . ."

"Yes, you're right. I no longer believe that he is a man of position or even that he is in Cairo. But he might be in any one of the other governorates. Not necessarily Cairo."

"You say you saw him yesterday?"

"I thought so. But I've lost faith in everything now."

"How long are you going to wait?"

"That's a good question. I can no longer afford searching, or waiting."

"And so?"

"I don't know. All the avenues seem to come to a dead end. I must return home and look for any job, or else . . . or else kill myself."

"And you say that you love me," she choked, biting her lips.

"Yes, Elham. I do. With every fiber in my being."

"And you talk of leaving and suicide?"

"Everything is lost now. I feel like someone slowly being strangled to death."

"But you love me. And I love you too."

Pain and hopelessness were all over his face. "But, Elham. I'm far beneath you."

"You must be patient, Saber," she pleaded. "I will stand by you."

"Oh, what's the use? I was dreaming when I thought I'd find my father. That's why I allowed you to enter my life. That's why I fell in love with you."

"Work. That's what will solve our problem."

"But I've already told you, there's nothing I know how to do."

"Give me a chance to think. You'll see, everything will turn out the way we want it to."

And what about the murder? How can things turn out for the better? It's all over now. How is it that the confession has not brought on the holocaust?

"Things won't turn out the way we want them to, Elham," he said quietly.

"Give me a couple of days," she said determinedly. "Don't make any decisions. I know what we want."

Tell her about your mother. Tell her what you did yesterday. Confess that you married another woman, a marriage that was sealed and consummated in blood. Tell her that you want to scream, scream, scream.

CHAPTER TWELVE

Here they are. The police and the calamity. Just as you had imagined all day long. The crime has been discovered, and only the criminal remains to be found.

There's no alternative but to go forward. Control yourself. Forget the look, the last look on Khalil's face. Forget also the last cry uttered by a dying man, a murdered man. The return to the hotel was a terrifying experience. Just like confessing. Your careful planning, useless. You should have left the hotel long before the crime. Enough of this dithering. The beggar, still singing despite everything. He made his way through the crowd of onlookers. A policeman stopped him.

"What happened? I'm a resident here." He saw Sawi, his face tear-stained and pale. "What happened, Sawi?"

Sawi burst into tears. "Mr. Khalil has been murdered!"

"Murdered!"

"He was found murdered in his bed. God's curses on the killer."

The lobby was crowded with policemen and detectives. In Khalil's chair sat the senior officer, and on his right, in Karima's chair, was another man. The senior officer was busy looking through some papers. One of the guests was sitting opposite the officer. The officer reminded him very much of his father. He felt suddenly weak at the thought but then noticed that the officer was a much younger man. How silly, he thought; everyone seems to look like my father. Should he wait or go straight to his room? He was just about to go upstairs when the man sitting in Karima's chair said, "Please wait in the lounge."

He walked into the lounge and sat with a group of hotel guests. "What happened?" he asked.

"Mr. Khalil was found murdered."

"How?"

"Who knows? The police have asked us all to stay here for the investigation. They've searched everywhere."

He heard subdued, choking sobs. There in the opposite corner of the lounge sat Karima. She was sitting between an old woman and an elderly-looking man. How could he have not noticed her when he entered? What should he do? After some hesitation he went over to her. "My profoundest sympathies, madam. You must be strong."

She didn't look up, but continued to sob. He went back to his corner, shaking his head as though in shock at the crime. Was it a mistake, what he just did? Could this old woman be the mother of the Alexandria sweetheart? What are the police thinking? Did they inquire about the resident in room thirteen? Was he already the subject of investigation? Do they understand criminals, as he understands loose women? He hated them all. Hated them to the point of killing!

"What now?" he asked the group.

"You've only been here a few minutes. We've been here since morning."

"Have they questioned the other guests?"

"Yes, and they let them go. Our turn has not come yet. They also questioned the wife, her mother, and her uncle."

"But I believe she wasn't here."

That was rash! The guest continued: "That makes no difference. This place is full of surprises. They found a large amount of hashish in room six, and they arrested the man living there. Also, in room three they discovered a professional thief."

"Ah. Maybe."

"Yes, that's quite possible. It all depends on the motive."

"No doubt it was theft."

Again rash. You'd better be careful. Did they find any evidence? he wondered. He wanted to be with Karima, if only for a moment. Don't look in her direction. She must have some important information for him. It's not as you imagine. Damn that beggar and his incessant chant. I visit my mother at this time every month.

Money and jewelry are missing. Aly Seriakous closed the windows in front of me. I locked up myself. No. I don't think he has enemies.

Why does this man remind him of his father? A guest interrupted his thoughts. "We are innocent, and yet we're nervous and on edge. What must the guilty feel?"

Said another, "What's worse, that one false slip or a wrong expression can start endless troubles."

"But never was an innocent hanged."

"Hah!"

But the guilty may escape. Your mother and the man who escaped to Libya. You were mad to return to the hotel. There must have been some other way. Your need for your father becomes more urgent with the growing danger.

The guests were called one by one. His turn came. He sat before the investigator, hating him intensely. He must defeat him at all costs. The man looked at Saber's identity card.

"You've been here for over a month, as the hotel register shows."

No, he doesn't resemble his father. "I got up as usual, got dressed, and came down to have my breakfast."

"Not exactly as usual. You woke up early."

"I don't wake up at a set hour."

"The porter said that on this particular morning you were up earlier than usual."

"Probably he didn't see me on other occasions."

"Did you hear anything unusual at night?"

"No. I slept soundly the moment I got back to my room."

"Did you notice anything unusual when you woke up?"

"No."

"When did you see the porter, Aly Seriakous?"

"On my way out of the bathroom."

"Did he seem somewhat different to you?"

"No. He looked just as he does every day."

"And you? Tell me, is there anything about yourself that you haven't told me?"

"No."

"Didn't you forget your wallet?"

"Yes, yes. I did. Aly Seriakous brought it to the lounge."

"What impression did you have then? I mean after getting the wallet?"

"Naturally, I was pleased."

"What else?"

"That's all."

"Weren't you surprised at his honesty?"

"Maybe. I don't remember. It probably didn't occur to me."

"But it's natural that it should occur to you."

"Perhaps I was slightly surprised."

"Slightly?"

"I mean, I wasn't astounded or anything like that."

"How honest do you think he is?"

"I never noticed anything about him that would suggest dishonesty."

"Where did you go from the time you left until your return?"

"Walking about, here and there."

"No job, of course. That's clearly stated on your identity card. But also no friends?"

"I have no one here in Cairo."

"Yesterday. When did you leave the hotel?"

"Around ten in the morning."

"When did you return?"

"At midnight."

"You didn't return at any time during the day?"

"No."

"Is that your usual habit?"

How did you change your regular pattern yesterday? Why?

"I've done it maybe once or twice."

"Nobody here recalls that."

"But I do!" he said indignantly.

"Once or twice, you say?"

"Probably twice."

"And how do you spend your day, then?"

"Walking around. I'm a stranger here, and everywhere I go is new to me."

"What did you find upon your return?"

"I saw the doorman, Mohamed el-Sawi, here, and the porter, Seriakous, in front of the door of my room."

"What was he doing?"

"He asked me if I needed anything."

"Did you meet any of the other residents?"

"No."

"What did you do yesterday from ten in the morning until midnight?"

"I walked until lunchtime."

"Where did you have your lunch?"

"I had a sandwich at the grocer's on Clot Bey Street."

"Strange for someone of your means."

His hatred for this officer grew intensely. "I came across this grocer when I first arrived. You might say I became attached to him."

"Then what did you do?"

"I walked along the Nile."

"In this weather?"

"I'm from Alexandria, remember," he said, laughing, trying to conceal his fear and anger.

"Then what?"

The café? No. He must not drag Elham into all this. In Alexandria I saw the film showing at the Metro Cinema here. "I went to the Metro Cinema," he said quickly.

"When?"

"At six o'clock."

"Which film was showing?"

"On Top of the Clouds."

"And after nine, what did you do?"

"I walked around as usual. I also took the Heliopolis bus to the end of the line. Just to kill time." Kill! What a choice of words.

"Where did you have dinner?"

Be careful! "At the cinema. I had a sandwich and some chocolate."

"Did you meet anyone?"

"No."

"You know no one here?"

"No one." He paused a while, then added: "I contacted the advertising manager of the *Sphinx* newspaper. Purely business, you know." Was that a mistake? Could it implicate Elham?

"Why did you come from Alexandria to Cairo?"

"A visit. Tourist, you might say."

"But this hotel is not appropriate for a tourist of your means."

"It's very economical."

"Do you really possess private means?"

"Yes, of course."

"Tourism, is that the real purpose of your visit?"

The circle is closing. Lies will get you nowhere now. You never expected these questions when you planned all this. "I do have another purpose, apart from tourism."

"Tell me."

"It's family business."

"Tell me something about the property you own."

"Just money."

"No land or buildings?"

"Just money, cash."

"And your address in Alexandria. Is it what is stated on your identity card?"

Questions. Investigations. His home, the nightclubs. Basima Omran. You will invite suspicion, you cannot escape it.

"Yes, that's where I live."

"Which bank do you use?"

"Bank?"

"Yes. Where is your money deposited?"

"I don't use banks."

"Where do you keep your money?"

"In ... in my pocket."

"Your pocket? Aren't you afraid you might lose it?"

"There's very little left," he said quietly, with bitterness.

"But your identity card points out that you are wealthy."

"I was."

"What are you planning to do?"

Don't hesitate. I'll challenge him with the truth, or in spite of it.

"I was searching for my father. That's my future."

"You're looking for your father?"

"Yes. He left us when I was just a baby. I told you I had family problems; they're of no importance, not worth mentioning. Now that I've gone through my money, I've no recourse but to look for him."

"Have you any idea where he might be?"

"No. The advertisement in the newspaper is my last hope."

"Maybe that's the real reason why you are here in Cairo."

"Perhaps."

"How long will your money last?"

"A month at most."

"May I?"

With mounting but restrained anger, Saber handed him his wallet. The officer looked through it and then gave it back. "What are you going to do when the money runs out?"

"I was planning on finding a job."

"What are your qualifications?"

"None."

"What kind of a job?"

"Any kind of commercial enterprise."

"Do you think that'll be easy?"

"I've got friends in Alexandria; they will help me."

"Do you owe the hotel money?"

"No. I paid this week in advance."

"How did you find this hotel?"

"Purely by chance. I was looking for a cheap place to stay."

"Did you know anyone in this hotel before coming?"

"No."

"But since then? You know many people here, no doubt?

"Mohamed el-Sawi, Aly Seriakous."

"Mr. Khalil, I mean. The deceased, Khalil Abul Naga?"

"Naturally."

"What did you think of him?"

"A very old, very kind man."

"And yet someone saw fit to kill him."

"That's very sad."

"Did you know where he lived?"

"In a flat on the roof, I think."

"You're not sure?"

"No."

"How do you know?"

"Aly Seriakous told me."

"Or did you ask him?"

"Perhaps."

"I wonder why."

"I don't really remember. I usually chatted with the porter whenever I saw him."

"Did you ask him any other questions?"

His heart beat violently. "Perhaps. I cannot recall any specific questions. It was ordinary conversation, you know."

He felt the trap closing. The officer asked, "How long are you staying in Cairo?"

"Until I find my father or a job, or until my funds dry up."

The officer lit a cigarette and took a deep puff, then asked, "Have you anything else to add?"

"No."

"We might require you later; please don't leave without informing us."

"Yes, of course."

What an idiotic, incomplete scheme it was. Escape now would be madness. You'll be watched every minute of the day. You'd better think back over every question and try to find out where you stand.

CHAPTER THIRTEEN

Your position is precarious, obscure, just like death. Most probably they are already investigating you, watching you closely, your every move. You won't realize it. Just like Khalil before the fatal blow. Weigh your every move. You cannot afford a false one. The hotel is quieter now. The smell of death drove many of the guests away. But others will come. The lounge is cold, cold as the grave. Nothing new in today's paper. Talk about cotton, currency, and war. The wind howling outside as though chorusing the perpetual chant of the beggar.

He heard footsteps, looked up, and saw Sawi greeting Karima. He felt his stomach turn with emotion. Karima sat down with her old mother and Sawi. Did she come to take over the hotel? Will their eyes meet? He felt much better seeing her. When will we meet? Somehow she'll contact you. She's even more beautiful and sensuous in her mourning dress.

You're in desperate need of her passionate condolences, consoling you in your plight. She was talking quietly to Sawi. He heard him say, "I don't know when they'll allow us to enter the flat."

Where is she staying? It would be insane to follow her. How could you have possibly overlooked asking her mother's address? She must contact you by phone. She must remember how badly you're in need of money.

"Telephone, Mr. Saber."

Damn the telephone. What now? Has Reheimy perfected the

art of mocking me? He walked to the telephone and, passing her, offered his hand. "I repeat, Madam, my sincerest condolences."

She shook his hand without looking up. He kept his eyes on her while speaking on the phone.

"It's Elham, Saber."

Why isn't it Reheimy? Why did I come to Cairo? Why this hotel in particular?

"How are you, Elham?"

"Are you all right?" She sounded anxious.

"Yes, thank you."

"Why didn't you come yesterday?"

"I'm sorry. I was rather tired."

"Well, I won't reproach you now. You're coming today?"

"No, not today. As soon as I get rid of my cold."

"Well, I won't trouble you. You know where to find me." She seemed hurt.

"Goodbye."

"Goodbye." He didn't put the receiver down but pretended to continue with the conversation, looking straight at Karima.

"You must contact me in any way. By telephone perhaps."

She turned her eyes; she must have gotten the message.

"I want to know several things," he continued. "I am sure that you are aware of my situation; we must talk, and don't forget that my money is running out."

She gave him a warning glance. "I'm fully aware of your problems," he added quietly, "but I'm sure you'll find a way." He walked back to his seat in the lounge, feeling slightly relieved although still very worried. Karima got up, followed by her mother. He felt that he was seeing her for the last time. The crime was meaningless without her. He waited, hoping for that phone call. No call. A terrible silence was left in her wake. The lounge was empty except for him. He noticed Sawi looking at him, so he nodded to him, smiling.

The man asked, "Why are you here all alone?"

"It's my cold. I've taken a couple of aspirins. I'll go out if I feel better." He moved to the chair that had been occupied by Karima and sat down. "The telephone has driven me to utter despair."

"Well, I'm sure there must be a good reason for his not calling."

Saber looked at Sawi and said with some sympathy, "You've been going through very hard times."

The old man's face contorted with pain and sorrow. "May you never go through what I'm going through."

"It must have been a terrible sight. I've never seen a dead body before. Even my mother, I closed my eyes."

"Yes, but murder, that's something else."

"Yes, that's true. Murder, blood, savagery."

"Unbelievable savagery. No punishment is sufficient."

"I've often asked myself, what would drive a person to murder?"

"Yes, I wonder."

"And the murderer. What kind of person can he be?"

"I saw a murderer once, an errand boy. I had always thought he was so kind and gentle."

"Incredible."

"Yes, but what can we do?"

"How true. What can we do? We'll soon hear that he's been arrested."

The old man looked sadly at him. "He already has been arrested."

"Who?"

"The killer."

"The killer! But we didn't hear anything about it."

The old man nodded.

"Who is it?" asked Saber almost in a whisper.

"Aly Seriakous."

"That . . . that idiot."

"Just like the errand boy."

"Is that why I didn't see him around yesterday evening or today?"

"My God have mercy on us all."

"Has the wife been informed?"

"Naturally."

"Man is truly an enigma."

"They found the money on him."

"It could have been his money."

"He confessed to the theft."

"And to the murder?"

"I don't know."

"But you just said that they've arrested the murderer."

"That's what Karima said."

"Does that mean that theft was the motive?"

"I think so."

"He could have stolen without killing."

"Probably Mr. Khalil woke up and saw him, so he had to kill him."

"He was kind to the point of idiocy almost."

"As you said, man is an enigma."

"He's more than that," said Saber.

"Did you know that the poor beggar we hear singing every day was once the tough guy around here?"

"That decrepit old man?"

"He lost everything, money, health, his sight. He had no other recourse but to beg."

"But Aly Seriakous showed great honesty when he returned my wallet, which I had misplaced."

"He's smarter than we think."

Do such things happen so easily? Or is it purely our imagining based on emptiness? Nothing, nothing at all.

"Wouldn't it have been easier for him to escape?"

"Escape would be tantamount to confession."

"How could he have hidden the stolen articles in his room?"

"Maybe they found them at his home."

"Taking them there would have been foolish."

The old man sighed. "Such is the will of the Almighty."

"When I saw him the morning of the crime—before it was discovered, that is—he appeared calm and pleasant as usual." Saber's heart was pounding.

"Some people kill and attend their victim's funeral!"

Be careful. Don't let your hidden fears surface. The telephone might throw some light on matters.

The old man continued, still in a sad, tired voice: "I was the first to be questioned by the police."

"You?"

"Yes, of course. I was the last to see him alive last night and the first to enter his apartment this morning."

"But who could think . . . ?"

"I was bombarded with questions. I had closed the door myself. The windows were shut, but I found a window ajar."

"Maybe he forgot to close it."

"No. She insisted that all the windows were closed."

"Did Seriakous break in?"

"No, that's impossible. The noise would have woken everybody up, certainly Mr. Khalil."

"Maybe he knocked on the door and Mr. Khalil opened it."

"But why open the window? And also it was established that he was killed in his sleep."

Saber stared in silence. Then he said somewhat hopefully, "Maybe he hid in the bedroom?"

"No. He left the apartment before me. I locked up myself."

"Well, maybe . . ." The sentence died abruptly. It was stifled by a sudden fear. He was about to say that maybe Seriakous pretended that he was closing the windows. He is not supposed to know that Seriakous closed the windows. That was a close shave! It left him ice cold with fear.

"Maybe what?" the man asked.

"Maybe he used another key to open the door."

"Possibly. But why open the window?"

"It is most probable that they were left open. Forgotten."

"God knows."

"It must have been hard on you," Saber said sympathetically.

"I don't understand how they let me go. But they know their job."

"There's no more talk of the murder in the papers. All news stopped suddenly."

The old man was close to tears. "May God rest your soul, Mr. Khalil. I knew him for sixty years."

"How old was he?"

"Over eighty."

"When did he marry?"

"Ten years ago."

"It's a strange marriage, don't you think?"

"He married when he was young. He had a child; then suddenly, tragically, he lost his family. He remained single for a long time until she came along. He loved her as a father would his daughter, above anything else."

"That sounds reasonable, considering."

"He was a good man, kind and generous. He helped me raise and educate my children."

"How did he get married?"

"He used to travel frequently to Alexandria."

"Alexandria! Is she from Alexandria?"

"No. He used to stay with a friend of his who lived in Tanta. She was married at that time."

"Married?"

"Yes, to her cousin, a good-for-nothing. He met her at this friend's."

I am talking too much. "How did they get married?" Saber's curiosity made him reckless in his questions.

"She got a divorce, and they were married."

"She married a man over seventy?"

"Why not? He gave her honor and security."

"And peace of mind," Saber interjected heavily. He remembered his mother's last words. "But a good-for-nothing, as you describe her ex-husband, wouldn't divorce such a beautiful woman. Why did he divorce her?"

"Everything has its price." The old man immediately regretted this remark.

Saber noticed and said quickly, "Anyway, those things are past."

"I've said more than I should. Ever since I saw him lying in his blood, I'm not myself. May God forgive me."

A pimp's whore. A purchased slave. A coolheaded criminal, a vessel of unbelievable pleasures, your torturer to the end. Groundless intuition, nothing else, led you to this bloody hotel and flung you into crime, murder, blood. Just like the intuition that made you chase the car like a maniac.

CHAPTER FOURTEEN

Coffee and more coffee to alleviate the rigors of a sleepless night. He watched the telephone through a cloud of cigarette smoke. When will Karima ring? A heavy downpour lasted for a few minutes, leaving the streets soaked and muddy. Karima, silent as the dead, not realizing his agony. Heavy drinking, sleepless nights, nightmares. All this will leave traces on you, easily observed by watchful eyes. As for Karima, she doesn't care. One of the residents approached his table and asked if he might share it with him. The lounge was very crowded. He must be the last of the residents who were here when it happened. Obviously he is seeking some juicy gossip.

"They've arrested the killer," the man said.

"Yes, I know," said Saber, hiding his fear and annoyance behind a smile.

"Aly Seriakous?"

"Yes."

"Theft was the motive, I believe," said the man, settling comfortably into his chair. "I was wrong."

"What did you think?"

"Well, to be quite frank, I always suspect women."

Saber looked at him sharply; he continued: "A beautiful young woman who stands to inherit a good-sized fortune."

"I thought of the same thing," said Saber, feeling his nerves almost twanging with fear. Did the investigator think the same? But Karima is silent, like death. The telephone does not ring.

The rain, cold, and mud haven't silenced the beggar's singing. Mohamed el-Sawi called him, pointing to the telephone. He got up and moved toward it with heavy, tortured steps.

"Hello?"

"Saber?"

Never did he think that he would hear her voice while in such a state of despair. "Elham. How are you?"

"Am I disturbing you?"

"No. No. You'll see for yourself I've been sick. I'll wait for you today."

He must get her out of his life, no matter how painful it is. He must get her out of the mud he is floundering in. They met. There she was, ignorant of everything, smiling reproachfully. How could he love so deeply and sincerely?

"Don't you feel guilty?" she asked, smiling. He couldn't answer. She took off her gloves and sat down.

"That cold must really have affected you."

"It was a nasty bout with the flu."

"And no one to take care of you?"

"No one at all."

"Did you see a doctor?"

"No. I just let it run its course."

"Good. You must drink a lot of juice. It's good for you."

They ate in silence, her eyes never leaving him.

"I thought many times of coming to visit you."

"Thank God you didn't," he almost snapped.

She shrugged her shoulders, but didn't pursue the matter further. Then, full of enthusiasm, she said, "I haven't wasted a minute."

Oh! The pain you cause, Elham! Why don't you go away?

"You're an angel," he said quietly.

"Don't you believe me?" she chirped, her eyes dancing with joy. "Well, you're about to start ... *we* are about to start a new life. What do you say to that?"

He tried desperately to overcome his gloom. "I say that you are an angel, and me, I'm a crippled beast."

"The capital you need," she continued, undaunted, "is now available."

"Capital?"

"Yes. All that I've saved for the future. Also some of the jewelry I never wear. It's not a fortune, but it's quite sufficient. I asked people in the know, and believe me, we'll start out on solid ground."

Are such miracles possible? In your wildest dreams you never thought this could happen. Money without crime, and love to top it all. Resurrect the old man and awaken from your nightmare! He sighed woefully. "Elham, the more you do for me, the more I'm convinced that I'm not worthy of you."

"Stop trying to be a poet. There's no time."

Her happiness is burning like a bright flame. To extinguish it will be your second crime. But she is reaching out for something that does not exist. You never dreamed that there was such a simple solution to your problems. Well, there you have love, freedom, honor, peace of mind. And where do you stand? So much, so late.

"Why are you so pensive? I expected you to jump with joy."

The time has come! "I told you many times that I was not worthy of you; why didn't you believe me?"

"I expected you to jump with joy."

"It's too late," he almost wailed.

"Oh my God, you don't love me."

"Elham. Things are much more complicated. I loved you at first sight. But who am I?"

"Don't tell me about your father, your poverty, or your worthiness."

Oh, the hell I'm going through. There's no other way but to tell the truth.

"You are still suffering from the flu. You're sitting with me, but where is Saber? The Saber I knew when we first met?"

"Don't ever ask that question again."

"If you're ill . . ."

"No. It's not illness."

"Then what, what? What is the matter? Why did you say it's too late?" She was very close to tears.

"Did I say that?"

"Just a few seconds ago."

"I mean only one thing. I'm not worthy of you."

"Don't be idiotic. I love you," she said angrily.

"That's my crime. Unfortunately we thought only of love."

"And why is that a crime?"

"Because I should have told you the truth about myself."

"You did. And I accepted it."

"I spoke of my father, but . . ." Then bitterly he continued: But not about my mother."

She looked at him defiantly. "I love you, you. Your past has got nothing to do with it."

"You must listen."

"For God's sake, let her rest in peace."

"All of Alexandria knows what I'm going to tell you."

Then with vehemence mixed with bitterness and sorrow, he burst out: "She ended her days in jail!"

She started, disbelievingly, as if she were looking at a madman.

"Now do you understand?" Swallowing hard, he continued: "The government confiscated all her property, and that is the reason for my poverty. She left me with a hope that has destroyed me." The shock was brutal. But she'll recover. "I have no right to love someone like you. Only the loose women I've known all my life. But what could I do? I was helpless in my love for you."

She was silent. Struck dumb. That's good. No questions. Otherwise, you would have had to tell the whole story.

"My pure love for you is my only compensation. All my life I've spent in sin. It's the only thing I can do. Sin."

The biggest hurdle is now behind you. You almost feel happy. Oh, if only night wouldn't fall. Probably the investigator knows all these things by now. He got up and left without a word.

The telephone rang the following afternoon. "Elham!"

A low quivering voice said, "Saber. I just want to say that all you said yesterday, well, it doesn't change anything."

CHAPTER FIFTEEN

Elham. You're nothing but a constant torturing pain. As for Karima, you are linked in a bloody tie that will be broken only with death. Your need for her is like a maddening hunger that keeps you in a constant hell. You'll find a way of contacting her. You must!

The best thing we can do then will be to sell the hotel and live in some other town. You will lead a passionate, spontaneous, carefree life, not like Elham, whose voice calls for a change in your life and causes you endless pain. But when will Karima contact him? What happens after the money runs out? He would accept any job, even Seriakous', just to wait for Karima. I wonder, are they going to hang him? Poor Seriakous! You've killed a man with your own hands; no harm in killing another, but using different hands. When, when will this nightmare be over?

Before leaving the hotel, Elham telephoned him. "Are you going to renew the advertisement?" She sounded subdued.

"No," he replied wearily.

"I asked someone to find out if he's got an unlisted number," she said softly.

"And of course he didn't find anything."

"No, unfortunately."

"Don't worry about it," he sighed.

"We've got correspondents in other towns. They're inquiring as to his whereabouts."

"I don't know how to thank you, Elham."

"Aren't you thinking of coming to pay us a visit?" she asked shyly.

"No," he replied firmly. "I'm thinking of your welfare."

"I wonder how you are taking all this."

"I told you, it doesn't matter to me."

"It does to me," she whispered.

They lost contact after this. The pain was unbearable. What's the use of beauty in a world soiled with blood? Her eyes can only see what is beautiful. They are blind to ugliness.

Sawi saw him on his way out and smiled. Saber smiled back nervously. The man offered him a seat. He sat hiding his impatience and tension.

"Are you in a hurry?" asked the old doorman.

"No, not at all. I've got nothing to do."

"Then stay a while. To tell you the truth, I feel very lonely after the death of Mr. Khalil. I've no one to talk to."

"What about your sons?"

"They're not in Cairo."

There were only two guests in the lounge. The traffic noises drowned out the beggar's chant.

"Anything new turn up?" asked Saber.

"I've got a friend on the force. He seems to know, although he brags a bit."

"What does he say?"

"Aly Seriakous. They've found no one else."

"Perhaps he confessed?"

"I don't know."

"He was tempted by petty thievery."

"He denied the theft."

"But he had already confessed to it," Saber said, as though defending himself.

"Yes, but later he denied it."

"But they found the money at his home."

"He said the wife gave it to him."

"Mr. Khalil's wife?"

"Yes."

"But why?"

"Charity, maybe."

"But did she give charity to the other servants?"

"No. All the others were questioned. He's the only one."

"That's very strange," said Saber, swallowing hard.

"What is stranger still is that he then confessed again to the theft."

"And what about the so-called charity?"

"He said that she normally gave him tips for jobs that she wanted done. He saw where she kept the money, and this tempted him."

"He went to steal, and he killed."

"That's it, I think."

"What does the investigator think?"

"Who knows? But they seem convinced that he's the murderer."

"He has probably confessed," Saber said hopefully.

"Probably."

"No doubt the lady used to tip him."

"Perhaps."

"But why did he deny it and then confess?"

"Who knows?"

"There must be another facet to the problem."

"Ah. Who can be sure?"

For the first time he inspected the old man's face. Green, faded eyes. The closer he looked, the more he felt that he was seeing a new face, forgetting the old one. "Do you think that there is another facet?" asked Saber.

"How can I know?" replied Sawi, showing no interest in the matter.

Yes! That's how men will feel approaching the gates of hell! "You know much more than you're willing to tell," said Saber cunningly.

"I'm afraid that the opposite is more correct."

"Did they ask the wife any more questions?"

"The officer called her more than once."

"Did Seriakous' statement have anything to do with that?"

"Yes."

"Do you have confidence in your friend? The one who gave you this news?"

"But she said so herself."

"The wife?"

"Yes. She was here yesterday evening."

She chose a time when he would be out! That cunning, wicked devil! Of what consequence can the investigation be compared with his predicament? Beware; the old man might read more than just curiosity into your questions. But how can I avoid these burning questions?

"Did she speak about her gift to Seriakous?"

"Yes, it was only charity, of course."

"That's reasonable."

"Why?"

"Aly Seriakous doesn't strike me as a man ..."

"Are you aware of these things?" asked Sawi.

"Not every man is capable."

"But I've lived far longer than you," said the old man.

"Are you doubting her character?"

"I didn't say that."

"Then you are confident she's honest?"

The old man closed his eyes sadly. "I don't doubt her, I know."

Observe how matters are being revealed. Your investigation is proving more successful than the real investigation!

"Then she is dishonest?"

"Unfortunately . . . Yes . . ."

"Did you know this before your friend's death?"

"Yes. But I cared for his peace of mind more than the truth."

"Did you give your opinion in the investigation?"

"Of course."

"You mentioned the relationship between her and Aly Seriakous?"

"Aly Seriakous . . . I'm not thinking of him."

Was this the trap? And had he fallen for it? "We were talking about him."

"Yes, but then we talked about her."

"As the other party."

"No. There is another man."

Can her fires consume more than one man? Of course they can! It is known as hell!

"Another man?"

"Her previous husband."

"The man who sold her," said Saber breathlessly.

"It was merely a business deal."

"But how do you know all this?"

"I saw him several times at her mother's house when I was there."

Hell's gates were opened wide. "And you didn't mention it to anyone?"

"It would have killed my master to know."

"He was killed in spite of it."

"Yes, and that's the tragedy."

"Why did he allow those visits?"

"His age destroyed his ability to doubt."

"You also mentioned this during the investigation?"

"I did."

"Did they question the other man?"

"He was not in Cairo on the night of the murder."

"That doesn't preclude that he planned it."

"Yes, that's true. But they let him go."

"Why?"

"They have their reasons, I suppose."

"They must have used the servant with incredible cunning."

"Or some other idiot like him."

Saber swallowed hard. "Maybe these are all groundless doubts."

"Perhaps," said Sawi, noncommittally.

"But you said that you're sure."

"Maybe I used the wrong expression."

"Well, we're back where we started."

The old man shook his head gravely. "My heart tells me that my doubts are well founded."

"But there might not be any connection between her adultery and the crime."

"That's possible. Otherwise they wouldn't have let them go."

"In any case, Seriakous has served them well," said Saber spitefully.

"If he's the murderer."

"Do you doubt that?"

"Everything is possible."

"Sometimes I think that you don't believe it."

"And why not? You remember what I told you about that errand boy?"

"Maybe he's the killer."

The old man sighed. "I think that the killer will strike again. Perhaps not right away. But he'll strike again."

You'll not sleep a wink until you question her yourself. What a devil of a woman. But she'd be a fool if she thinks she can trick you. She knows that you can kill. But how to find her?

"Her previous husband," said the old man, "didn't plan the murder. Otherwise they wouldn't have let him off so quickly. But the other crime . . ."

"He's her cousin," Saber interrupted, "and it's not strange that he should visit her."

"Actually, I had my doubts long ago. Her mother used to live very near here, and her husband would take her there whenever she wanted. Then suddenly the mother moved to number twenty Sahil Street, in Zeitoun, miles away. Why? I could find no logical reason except that the wife could use it as an excuse to spend some days at her mother's. Mr. Khalil objected at first, but then gave in."

How easy it all was! Number twenty Sahil Street, Zeitoun. No effort at all.

Saber was now lost in a raging tempest of madness. The smell of blood was strong in his nostrils.

CHAPTER SIXTEEN

He knew he was being watched; otherwise he would have gone immediately to Zeitoun. Patience and a plan were both required. Sawi was sitting in the old man's, the dead man's, chair. For a moment Saber thought it was Khalil, then for the first time the truth of his actions hit him with a ferocious impact: he had taken a life.

I wonder if Khalil is thinking of me now? If he can, what thoughts must be passing through his mind?

He greeted Sawi, who returned the greeting quickly and looked back into the register, as though he had forgotten yesterday's conversation.

He took his breakfast in the lounge, halfheartedly, without any appetite. Karima. No one is going to make a fool of me. Karima will not escape me. She can try what she will, but the hangman's rope is in my hands. Nothing seemed changed in the lounge, the same chatter about war and money, and outside, the beggar chanting. Elham was on the phone.

"Can I see you today just for a few minutes?"

"I can't."

"Give me a good reason why not."

"I can't."

"Even if it has to do with your father?"

"My father?"

"Yes."

"What do you mean?"

"Let's meet today."

"I can't." Even his father could not save him from the whirlpool of his fury.

"But it's about your father. The object of your search."

"So what?"

"Shall I come?"

"No," he said impatiently. What news could she have? Anyway, what difference is it to him now? Zeitoun, that's the objec-
tive. His father. That was probably a trick to get him to see her.
He drank heavily. Cheap wine. Walking around trying to think
of a plan to fool the watchful eyes.

I'll go up to my room. But I shall not sleep. The detective
will. At dawn, he crept slowly downstairs. A servant was sleeping in the lobby in front of the door, the locked door. He dared
not wake the man up. He might be the detective. Slowly, he
went back up the stairs. Suddenly an idea occurred to him.
He raced up the stairs, all the way to the roof. A shiver ran
through him as he passed the closed apartment. He crossed the
roof to the wall of the adjoining building, and without hesitating
for a second, jumped over to the building. Breathing heavily,
he went down the stairs to the entrance. The doorman's room
was closed. The front door was closed. Damn! Nothing but ob-
stacles. He tried the key that was in the lock. It didn't work.
Why? He tried the door handle. It worked. The door wasn't
locked. Why? He opened the door slowly, quietly. Suddenly a
man blocked the now open doorway. "Who's there?" a voice
cried.

Without hesitation, he drove his fist violently into the man's
face and kicked him in the stomach as he doubled up. The man
fell, silent, motionless. He rushed out into the cold empty dawn.
Crossing the street quickly and racing toward the square. Without warning, he collided with something.

"Oh! Help! Please, please, I'm blind."

"I'm sorry, it's very dark," he said as he hurried on. He shuddered. That cursed beggar. Ubiquitous.

The taxi drove toward Zeitoun. The detective is going to have a long wait. He got out of the cab at the beginning of Sahil Street. He walked toward the small bungalow. Daybreak was slowly filtering through the dark.

He knocked on the front door, not caring what lay ahead. Karima! There she was, just as she appeared on her first nocturnal visit. He pushed past her.

"Are you mad?"

They faced each other under a bare, glaring lamp.

"You must be insane."

"Maybe." He looked at her with his bloodshot eyes.

"Don't you realize the consequences of your action?"

"It's better than waiting without hope," he hissed.

"You must wait. Don't you see that my situation is far more critical than yours?"

"And how long must I wait? Till death? Why didn't you phone?"

"Sawi would have recognized my voice."

"Anyone could have spoken instead of you."

"They asked me so many questions. I panicked."

"You panicked? You who plot murders in bed while making love?"

"Don't raise your voice. My mother's asleep."

"Isn't she your accomplice?"

"You're mad. You look so strange."

"I must see your bedroom."

"It's just like any other room."

"Don't be funny, I must see who shares it with you."

"Have you gone out of your mind?"

"Your cousin. Your previous husband. Isn't he here?" he shouted.

"Who said so? No one is here. You've brought disaster upon us now by coming here."

"I don't care. I must see for myself."

He pushed her roughly out of his way and opened the first door he saw. An old woman was fast asleep. Another door, another bedroom. Hers, most probably. He searched every room. No trace. "You've driven me crazy," he cried, returning to the hall. "You must avoid him during the investigation."

"Saber, I think someone is behind all this. Some cunning devil," she said, trying to calm him down.

"Weren't you married to your cousin?"

"I was."

"And didn't he sell you to the man you plotted to murder?"

"They'll arrest us, you fool. Today."

"Answer me."

"You're an idiot. I risked my life because I love you."

"He came to sleep with you in this ... whorehouse!"

"Can't you see the truth? Have you forgotten what was between us?"

"Every woman is an accomplished actress in bed."

"Please, please believe me. These are all lies!" She was almost hysterical.

"Do you think I'm afraid of hanging? I'll never leave you to another man."

"There is no other man. Believe me. If you don't, they'll get us before sunrise."

"Whore! Liar! You destroyed my life with a lie."

"Believe me, I beg you. I love you. All I've done is for your sake!"

"You destroyed me to enjoy the fruits of my crime with your lover."

"You are my lover! Believe me before it's too late. This man stepped out of my life years ago!"

"You divided things like only the devil can. I get the murder and you, the money."

"Oh, what's the use? We're finished. Once more, won't you believe me?"

"No."

"Then what do you want?"

"To kill you."

"And hang?" she screamed.

"I don't give a damn anymore!"

Several footsteps, followed by thunderous banging on the door. Karima screamed loudly, "The police! It's too late!"

He pounced on her savagely, blindly, his hands closing around her neck. Screams, the door banging, more screams, the door crashing open.

CHAPTER SEVENTEEN

And where now, Saber? In jail, alone. No one visits you. You have no one. Elham is now a distant dream, a vision. She must have gotten over her love. She must be cursing it!

The newspapers carry the full story, Karima, Mr. Khalil, Mohamed Ragab, her first husband. Your photograph. The wedding photograph, even Elham, and of course, Basima Omran. The papers leave no stone unturned.

But in jail you are liberated from the vicissitudes of life, just as in the womb. Saber, arrested while murdering his mistress. Saber, there's a story behind him. Basima Omran, queen of the Alexandria nightlife. She offered him in his poverty and despair an unknown father, a lost hope. The search for Sayed Sayed el-Reheimy. Love. Murder. Saber's amorous adventures and conquests. Saber, the symbol of cruelty and corruption. They admired his love for Elham. How noble that was in the midst of a sordid story.

His mother afforded him a brief life of luxury; when that inevitably collapsed, he had to find a father or kill. The investigator suspected you from the first. You were constantly watched. Sawi spoke to you of Karima's infidelity. That cunning old devil! What an idiot I've been!

Her first husband, Mohamed Ragab, denied any connection with the victim. It was the lover who fell in the trap. Was Ragab lying, or was he simply telling the truth? The papers don't give any details of the part that resulted in your destruction. Will you find out the truth after death?

Mohamed el-Sawi, the doorman, spun his web of lies which ensnared you in the trap. The address you got out of him so effortlessly. The doorman of the building who almost caught you on your way to her. The detective recognized your voice as you apologized to the beggar when you bowled him over. Curse that beggar!

The papers splash your scandalous life just as they do your mother's. A magazine made a study of your case. Learned men gave their opinions. Incompatible marriage between the old man and Karima. The prime cause of the murder. Poverty is the cause. Karima's first husband sold her because of poverty. Karima is the martyr of the class war. Saber's upbringing in a den of sin. Saber's Oedipus complex. In Karima he saw a mother substitute, and Khalil was a symbol of power, which he had to destroy.

He avenged the confiscation of his mother's wealth. It's a matter of a lost religious faith. If Saber had spent only a fraction of his efforts searching for God rather than searching for his father, none of this would have happened.

Saber shrugged his shoulders as he read all these comments. No one knows whether Karima was lying or telling the truth, or whether Reheimy existed or not, he told himself.

A lawyer called one day to see Saber. He thought he'd seen him somewhere before. But where and when, he could not remember. He felt comfortable in the lawyer's presence. He was an elderly, distinguished-looking man.

"Are you the lawyer chosen by the court to defend me?"

"No." Then, in a quiet voice, the lawyer said, "I am Mohamed el-Tantawi."

Saber did not recognize the name. "Who gave you my case?"

"Consider me your friend."

"But I have no money."

The man smiled. "I'm Ihsan Tantawi's elder brother. You know, the advertising manager of the *Sphinx*."

"Oh! I see. I thought I had seen your face before." Then sadly he asked, "Are you going to defend me?"

"Yes. If you'll allow me."

Suddenly Saber cried out, "Elham!"

The lawyer smiled but did not say anything.

"What about your fee?"

"Just the necessary expenses."

Was it possible? Her love paying for his funeral!

"I'm afraid you'll be wasting your time, sir."

"The word 'hopeless' does not exist in our dictionary."

"But I killed two people, premeditated murder, confessed."

"And so . . ."

"And Elham. Why?"

"You don't have relatives, but that doesn't mean you don't have a friend."

"Even after I confessed?"

"She accepts that."

He wiped at his tears. "The second tear in my life."

"There's nothing wrong with tears. Let's get down to business."

"I confessed everything."

"There are circumstances."

"What circumstances could possibly help me?"

"Your upbringing, love, jealousy, your feelings for Elham!"

"That'll only give the newspapers more fodder."

"We shall not give up."

"It's all like a strange dream. I came from Alexandria to look for my father, and then strange things happened which led me to forget my original purpose and finally drove me to jail." He sighed and continued: "And now I have forgotten everything else and only remember my original intentions. Well, there's not much use thinking about this now."

"I might use it in the defense. I will say that this was the first crime. A crime that took place before you were born."

"But now I remember something. Elham called me one day saying she had news about my father."

"What did she say?"

"I didn't see her. I was busy seeking revenge!"

"Well, I assure you, she knows nothing about him."

Saber shook his head, bewildered and in despair. "The crime coverage in the papers, that is the best possible advertisement. Maybe it will bring some results."

"I'm sure that any concern shown by your father now will make no difference whatsoever."

"Maybe if he turns up some miracle will happen."

"How?"

"If he really is important and influential."

"He cannot change the law."

"Listen, sir, my mother wielded influence once, and she was able to change the law right under the noses of the law-makers!"

"Well, please explain to me how your father could possibly help you."

Saber hesitated, then: "Escape maybe."

"Your imagination is running away with you! Stop thinking about these possibilities; it'll only bring on heartache."

"Well, in any case, sir, I thank you, and I'll be at your disposal in any way you wish. As for my wild hopes, well, sir, as you said, 'hopeless' is not a word in my dictionary!"

The judge pronounced sentence. Hanging. Saber followed the trial closely and expected his sentence. Nevertheless, he was stunned.

"We still have a chance to appeal," said the lawyer.

"How is Elham?" asked Saber dejectedly.

"Not so well. The story in the papers, it seems, brought her father back from Assiut, and he insisted on taking her back with him, for a change of air."

"So he crept out of his hole!" Saber cried out. "But my father . . ."

The lawyer smiled. "That reminds me. Would you believe that I have some news of your father?"

"No!"

"Yes." The lawyer continued: "Did you ever hear of a newspaper commentator who used to sign his column 'The Old Pressman'? Of course not; that was long before your time. He stopped writing twenty years ago. Well, he's my neighbor in Heliopolis. He was also my teacher at the Faculty of Law. We were talking about your case, and I mentioned your father. He then cut me short and said, 'Do you mean Sayed Sayed el-Reheimy? Well, I know him. The rich, handsome Reheimy. He was about twenty-five years old. That must have been over thirty years ago.' "

"But didn't your friend see the photograph in the paper?"

"He hasn't picked up a paper in twenty years. And besides, he's blind!"

"But the name, the description, the age."

"Yes, that's true."

"Where is he now?"

"I'm afraid he doesn't know."

"Did he tell you about my father's first marriage?"

The lawyer smiled. "He told me that his only pleasure was love."

"But my mother deserted him. Surely that's something he wouldn't forget."

"In the life of a man like Reheimy, women change daily. You can't distinguish between the deserter and the deserted."

"My mother never spoke to me about this aspect of his life."

"Maybe she didn't know about it."

"But you cannot hide marriage."

"My friend, Aly Borhan, I mean 'The Old Pressman,' said that he married, very frequently, all sorts of women, old, young, rich, poor, widowed, married, divorced, even maidservants and prostitutes."

"Amazing!"

"True."

"But didn't this pose problems?"

"Nothing stood in his way."

Saber could not believe his ears. "What work did he do?"

"He was a millionaire. Love was his sole profession. Every time he was trapped, he just moved away somewhere else."

"But my mother's marriage certificate, I've still got it."

"You'll probably find countless others."

"Was he never sued in court?"

"Who knows? He is divorced, that's quite sufficient."

"And what about the law?" said Saber sarcastically.

"He was never caught. Mr. Borhan said that once he had trouble with a virgin girl from a wealthy family. He left the country at the appropriate time."

"When did he return?"

"He didn't. The world became his playground. He could afford to pursue his hobby anywhere."

"How did your friend know all this?"

"They used to correspond occasionally."

"Does he have any idea where he might be now?"

"No. He never gave his address. And he never stayed too long in one place."

"He must be well known abroad."

"Every millionaire is well known. But he probably used different names. It's more prudent in his line of work!"

"When did your friend receive the last letter from him?"

"You know, my friend is over ninety now. He doesn't remember things too clearly. All he remembers is that he received letters from every corner of the globe."

"But he surely knows everything about his family."

"He has none in Egypt. His father was an immigrant from India. My friend knew his father, and through him, his only son, Sayed. The father died forty years ago, leaving his fortune to his sole heir. He made his fortune in spirits. He has no heirs in Egypt except those that may have resulted from his amorous adventures."

"Like me."

"Yes, like you, if he is really your father."

"I don't doubt it, now that you've told me of his habits."

The lawyer smiled and said nothing.

"Yes, his habits are my habits. But while he pursues them around the world, here I am in jail awaiting the hangman."

"But he didn't kill."

"Your old blind friend doesn't know everything," said Saber bitterly.

"In any case, he is a millionaire."

"What's more important is that the law cannot touch him."

"But you know that you are poor and subject to the law."

"And I also know who my father was."

"And to what avail?"

"Yes, unfortunately. My mother knew him better than your old friend. She made her fortune through him and was able to defy the law; she was unfortunate."

"But he never knew misfortune."

"It was impossible that I should have accepted work as a pimp after I discovered my true origin."

"Unfortunately, you did not live up to your origin."

"I looked for him."

"And forgot about him. You said so yourself."

"Because of a woman. He would understand that."

"But he is not your judge."

"But he is the one who deserted me."

"He might have thought that you were as capable as he, and didn't have any need of him."

"Had my mother not deserted him, maybe."

"But she did desert him."

"It's not my fault."

"That's true."

"That was the real reason for the crime."

"No. That's too farfetched."

"But it's a better reason than a chance meeting with someone like Karima."

"The law is the law."

Saber sighed deeply. "Maybe it would have been better if I denied that he's my father."

"That was my opinion. But I saw how eager you were to know anything about him."

"And what did I learn? Nothing useful."

The lawyer nodded.

"Everything is lost now; freedom, honor, peace of mind, Elham, Karima. Only the hangman's rope remains," he said with a deep sigh.

"We can still appeal," said the lawyer. "There's something else Mr. Borhan told me."

"What?"

"One day, to his surprise, Reheimy came knocking on his door!"

"What! When?"

"Last October."

"October!"

"Yes."

"I was searching in Alexandria at the time."

"He spent six days in Alexandria."

"This is utter madness! I asked everywhere about him. I didn't advertise in Alexandria; I was afraid that my enemies might make fun of me."

"Surely finding him was more important than worrying about mockery."

"Yes, yes! Oh, yes!" he wailed.

"Don't upset yourself. Maybe he didn't read the papers."

"Oh! Don't try to soften my despair."

"I'm sorry I told you all this." The lawyer watched Saber's agonized face, then, trying to comfort him, said, "He was on his way to India. He gave my friend a book on how to stay young for a hundred years. Also a case of the finest whiskey."

"Probably it was him in the car that night. Did he sign the book?"

"I think so."

"Can I see it?"

"I'll bring it."

"May I keep it for a while?"

"I don't think my friend would object."

"Thank you. What else did your friend say?"

"Mr. Borhan said that Reheimy was still as young and virile as he was thirty years back. He told him how he moved around the world and that he could not consider himself among the living unless he had made love in the four corners of the globe."

"Did he mention any of his offspring?"

"He might have. But he speaks only of love. They spent the evening drinking heavily, Reheimy telling his countless stories. He even sang a love song he had heard in the Congo."

"Drinking and singing and not a question about his sons?"

"Maybe fatherhood changes when it is practiced to excess."

"But sons remain sons, regardless of their number."

"Often strange contradictions occur when a strong father believes his sons will follow his example."

"What an excuse," said Saber scornfully.

"We forgive perverts deviations we wouldn't forgive others, so we would surely forgive someone like this incredible person."

"Oh! My head! It's spinning. I can't believe all this."

"I'm sorry I told you."

"Maybe he's still in Egypt."

"No. He sent a postcard from abroad."

"Maybe he'll visit me before I hang."

"Nothing is impossible."

"You know, I used to visit Elham and your brother Ihsan every week and little did I know then that I would one day be close to you, you the neighbor of Borhan, the friend of Reheimy."

"Sometimes life is like that."

"What a unique opportunity that could have been."

"There is still hope."

"How . . . what hope?"

"We might get you a life sentence instead of death."

"What hope!"

"You'll still have another opportunity to appeal."

"And if the appeal is quashed?"

The lawyer did not answer. He clenched and unclenched his fists nervously. Saber continued: "If the appeal is quashed, and I still have some time, please do me a favor and try to contact the man."

"My son, the law is the law. My duty lies in studying your case, not going on a wild-goose chase."

"But all you've heard of him, doesn't that convince you how strange he is?"

"I am a lawyer. I know that it is only the law that will decide your fate."

"There might be a chance. I might be foolish, but during the little time I've got, please do what I ask of you."

"I have no means of finding him."

"You are a man of experience. Your neighbor seems . . ."

"Contacting him is not impossible, but it requires a lot of time, one thing we haven't got. We must contact all our embassies abroad. He might have moved in the meantime."

The memory that is fading, dying away. So far and yet almost there, almost. The cloud formations in the sky, blown about carelessly in the wind. Pain tearing away at you behind prison bars. The blind questions leading to the oppressing answer. "It seems there's no use relying on anyone."

The lawyer smiled understandingly. "There is only use in what is reasonable."

Saber shrugged his shoulders and sighed. "Oh! Let anything happen now."

About the Author

The leading Arabic novelist, NAGUIB MAHFOUZ was born in Cairo in 1911 and began writing when he was seventeen. A student of philosophy and an avid reader, he has been influenced by many Western writers, he says, including Flaubert, Zola, Camus, Dostoyevsky, and above all, Proust. Until his retirement in 1972, Mahfouz worked in various government ministries—but he was always writing. Today he has more than thirty novels to his credit, among them his masterwork *The Cairo Trilogy*. He lives in the Cairo suburb of Agouza with his wife and two daughters.